"You can't tell me you haven't been wondering," Lucas murmured

"Wondering about what?"

"What it would be like. Me kissing you." His gaze drifted to her face, skimmed down to her lips. "You kissing me back."

"Lucas—" Grace warned, holding up a hand. "Don't you dare—"

"Too late." He gathered her close, covered her mouth with his, and took what he wanted.

Lucas had kissed other women before. More than he cared to count. But none of them had ever instantly fogged his brain as was happening now. He'd suspected she'd be sweet. And she was. Sweet and succulent and delicious. But he hadn't been prepared for the punch that followed the initial taste.

Uncharacteristically unsure of his footing, like a man backing away from the jagged edge of a steep precipice, he drew away, just far enough to see her eyes. They were dark and dazed and revealed both shock and a wariness he could identify with.

He wanted her. Worse yet, he needed her.

Even more important, he had to keep her safe....

Dear Reader,

I attended my first Romance Writers of America conference in 1982, my first *Romantic Times* conference in 1983, and have long been grateful for the friendship and support I've received from people in both these organizations. It's important to me that readers understand that the events taking place at the Romance Novelists' Network Conference portrayed in *1-800-Hero* are merely figments of my admittedly vivid imagination; no romance writers, agents, critics, editors, publishers, (even ex-husbands) depicted are even distantly inspired by any actual individual.

This is not a case of an ungrateful author biting the hand that feeds her, but rather a gently satirical look at a genre I love and respect. With that in mind, I do hope you enjoy Lucas and Grace's adventure in romance-convention land. And I hope you enjoy all the wonderful books in the HERO FOR HIRE miniseries.

Happy reading!

JoAnn Ross

1-800-HERO
JoAnn Ross

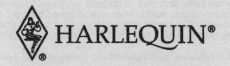

TORONTO • NEW YORK • LONDON
AMSTERDAM • PARIS • SYDNEY • HAMBURG
STOCKHOLM • ATHENS • TOKYO • MILAN • MADRID
PRAGUE • WARSAW • BUDAPEST • AUCKLAND

ISBN 0-373-25793-7

1-800-HERO

Copyright © 1998 by JoAnn Ross.

1

LATER, WHEN IT WAS all over, Lucas Kincaid would decide the entire adventure was proof that the gods did, indeed, laugh whenever men planned. In the beginning, however, he foolishly believed himself capable of controlling his destiny.

It was D-Day. Departure Day. This time tomorrow, he'd be cruising through the Pacific's blue water, headed for Alaska. There was no longer any reason to stay here in San Francisco. He'd successfully wrapped up his final case last night, when he'd put the English movie star back on the British Air jet to London. The past ten days spent dodging seduction attempts while accompanying the spoiled, sex-crazed actress on a publicity tour for her upcoming film had only confirmed Lucas's decision that he didn't belong in the bodyguard business.

He simply didn't have the people skills for the work. Part of the problem was that, despite his Southern upbringing, he'd inherited his grandmother Fancy's penchant for plain speaking. During his midshipman days at the naval academy, such outspokenness had resulted in being put on report for insubordination more times than he cared to count.

Another problem was his impatience with prima donna types. There'd been several occasions during this latest gig when Lucas had been tempted to spank the redhead, whose off-screen antics were even more outrageous than her sex-bomb movie roles.

"She probably would have enjoyed it," he muttered, thinking back on a few of the actress's kinkier sexual suggestions.

He finished emptying his desk, then stood at the window, took in the always riveting sight of the wide blue bay and the orange spans of Golden Gate Bridge, and contemplated leaving early. Since everyone had already taken off for the holiday weekend, the office was uncharacteristically as quiet as a Bible Belt whorehouse on Sunday morning. If he left now, he might be able cruise up the coast, dock at Petaluma and spend a lazy weekend enjoying the historic old town that had put arm wrestling on the map.

The phone rang. Lucas ignored it. He didn't need ESP to know it meant trouble. When it continued to ring, he felt the heavy yoke of responsibility—another damn Fancy inheritance—settle over his shoulders. He picked up the receiver.

"Kincaid."

"I was hoping I'd find you there."

He bit back a curse, glared out at the enticing span of San Francisco Bay gleaming in the late afternoon sun and once again considered escape. Then, surrendering to the inevitable, he threw himself into the leather chair and put his booted feet up on the desk.

"Well, hey there, darlin'." His friendly tone belied his aggravation. "Are you callin' to congratulate me on wrapping up the case of the British bimbette?"

"Good try, Kincaid," the female voice on the other end of the phone countered. "But you're not going to duck the issue."

"Well now, I can't rightly recall ever ducking anything in my life." There *had* been that bullet in Hawaii when the winsome hotel-dinner-show hula dancer had forgotten to mention a husband, but Lucas didn't figure that was relevant to this conversation.

"The issue, as you damn well know, is you trying to quit on me."

"But I have quit," he reminded her patiently. S. J. Slade was determined to keep him from leaving. Just as he was determined to leave. The battle of wills had been going on for the past month, despite the fact that he'd flat out told her there was no way he was changing his mind. "Our deal was that as soon as I put that redheaded barracuda on the plane, I was sailing off into the sunset."

"That was your deal, hotshot. Not mine."

"Heaven help me, I do love a contrary woman." He leaned back in the chair and switched the phone to the other ear. "Why don't you bail on the female executive gig you've got goin', Samantha darlin', and come sailing the seven seas with me?"

"One week out to sea and we'd undoubtedly be trying to drown one another."

"You may just have a point," he agreed with a chuckle. "But think of the high times we'd have for the first six days."

When he heard a snort he took for a smothered, reluctant laugh, Lucas figured he'd successfully defused the situation. He'd thought wrong.

"I've got a case for you."

"Now, I told you, sugar—"

"Don't sugar me," she retorted. "And quit talking like some uneducated Southern redneck right out of *Deliverance.* Don't forget, I've seen your resumé. You just happen to have dual degrees in literature and mathematics."

"I won't tell if you don't."

"Dammit, Lucas, this is serious."

"You wouldn't have called at the start of a holiday weekend if it wasn't." That was an out-and-out lie. The

sharp-tongued owner of the bodyguard agency Lucas
had been working for for the past eighteen months never
allowed Sundays, holidays or even what any normal person would consider sleeping hours to stop her from contacting her operatives. "And you know I admire you
greatly, darlin', but—"

"Why don't you knock it off with the buts until you
hear me out?" she snapped, cutting him off again. "And
get your damn cowboy boots off my antique desk."

Although they'd never met face-to-face—indeed, Lucas
didn't know anyone at the agency who'd actually ever
seen S. J. Slade in person—she knew him too well. "It's a
reproduction."

He crossed his feet at the ankles and admired the hand
tooling on his boots. That was the only problem with
boats: he couldn't wear his beloved Tony Lamas on board
because the heels scuffed the *Rebel's Reward*'s teak decks.
"But a very good reproduction," he allowed, glancing
around the office, which was decorated in an eclectic
blend of Chippendale furniture and black-and-white
movie posters.

The office, located on the third floor of the Victorian
Queen Anne building that housed the S. J. Slade Agency,
definitely reflected Samantha's fondness for 1940s detective movies. Although she'd assured him when he'd
come to work for her that he could make whatever
changes he wanted, Lucas hadn't bothered, since he
hadn't planned to stay in San Francisco all that long.

"Now you're an antique dealer," she grumbled.

"Actually, that's my mama who's the antique dealer."

"Dammit, you're doing it again. Getting me off track."

Despite his irritation, Lucas smiled at that idea. Samantha Slade was about as single-minded as a hound dog
scratching fleas. There was very little that could get her

off track. He'd always taken perverse pleasure in being able to.

"To get back to business, since the office is technically closed this weekend, I had my calls forwarded here," she said.

Lucas wasn't surprised. Samantha's workaholic lifestyle would have made the Puritans look like pikers. From what he could tell, the woman lived, slept and breathed the bodyguard business.

"We've got a priority-one call on the 800 line. From the *USA Today* ad."

He knew exactly what ad she was referring to, of course. Samantha Slade advertised her business in the classifieds all over the country: Need a Hero? Call 1-800-555-Hero. Personally, he'd always thought it embarrassingly cute. But he couldn't deny that it brought a lot of business into the agency.

"There's a convention in town this weekend," she revealed, blithely ignoring his ripe curse.

"Now there's a surprise."

"It's at the Whitfield Palace. The RNN's—otherwise known as the Romance Novelists Network's—annual bash."

"No way." He could see this one coming and would rather walk the plank than baby-sit some white-haired old lady swathed in pink chiffon and diamonds.

"It's right up your alley, sweetheart." Lucas hated it when Samantha called him sweetheart. Or worse yet, precious. It meant she was going into coaxing mode, which was even more dangerous than her Captain Bligh routine. "Two thousand women, Lucas. Women with romance on their minds. And you. Just think of the possibilities."

"I'd rather not." He might have been something of a ladies' man during his navy days, but any guy who'd get within a block of two thousand women all gathered in one place with romance on their minds could well be risking estrogen poisoning. "Besides," he reminded her yet again, "I've quit."

"So you keep saying. But how are you going to live with your conscience if someone knocks off romance's most beloved author while you're sailing into the sunset?"

"Now who'd want to do a nasty thing like that?"

"That's what Roberta Grace needs you to find out."

"Sorry, sweetheart, but I've got a hot date with some killer whales."

"Those whales migrate up and down the coast all the time," she murmured, in a vague way that told him she was just guessing. "You can always catch up with them later."

"Dammit, Samantha—"

"I need you on this one, Lucas." There it was again. That feminine wheedling he didn't buy for a minute. But that didn't make it any less effective. "This could well be a life-and-death situation. Somebody's been writing Roberta Grace threatening letters. This latest one said this conference would be her last.

"Now the letters could be the work of a crank. Or not. If you'd just help me out for this weekend, I'll double your pay, and when the conference is over and the writer leaves town without a scratch, I promise not to say another word about your foolish plan to resign.

"In fact," she said, with what Lucas took to be a burst of spontaneous inspiration, "if you still insist on leaving, I'll come to the dock to wave you off. And even spring for the bubbly for the bon voyage party."

"Why can't you get someone else to cover the lady? How about Val? Hell, she reads the stuff."

He recalled the day Eric Janzen, an agent recruited from the DEA, had made the mistake of giving Valerie

Brown a bad time about the novels with the suggestive covers. The former Oakland cop had calmly put down the paperback she'd been enjoying during her lunch break, aimed her semiautomatic Beretta 9mm at a point below Eric's belt and threatened to blow away any chances he might have for any romance in the future. After that, not a single male in the place had dared utter a word about Val's choice of reading material.

"Val's up in Washington State, baby-sitting a software mogul who's gotten more than a few people ticked off about his plot to take over the electronic world."

"Dean, then." Dean Phillips came from the blue suit, starched white shirt and neatly knotted tie ranks of the FBI. Since the guy's training had apparently included the ability to remain unrelentingly polite under stress, Lucas figured he'd be a natural for this gig.

"Dean's in Albuquerque on a fund-raising junket with some politician. And before you run through my entire roster of operatives, all I'm asking you to do is to run by the Whitfield Palace and meet the lady. Then, if you still want to leave, I swear I'll find a replacement and not do a thing to stop you."

And pigs would sprout wings and start dive-bombing the Bay Bridge, Lucas thought.

"You're an angel," she said in her brisk, staccato voice when he didn't immediately respond. "I realize that since you're going to be spending the next three days at the hotel, you'll need to go home and pick up some clothes. I've arranged for you to meet with the client in Neptune's Table—that's the oyster bar off the hotel lobby—at six."

"How am I suppose to spot her with two thousand women roaming all over the place?"

"You're the professional. I have absolute faith in your ability," Samantha said blithely. "Also, while I was talking on the phone with her, I did a quick Internet search on the other line. Her publisher is Penbrook Press, and if her photo on their web site is at all current, she's remarkably young to have achieved such success, I'd guess about twenty-six or -seven. She also appeared to be a large girl, with long, rather mousy brown hair."

"I doubt any other of those two thousand women fit that description," he muttered.

"You used to track down terrorists in jungles," Samantha noted, reminding him of his navy SEAL days, which he'd just as soon forget. "I can't believe you'd have that much difficulty locating one romance writer. Besides, if you can't manage to spot the woman yourself, she's famous enough that I'd imagine all you'd have to do is ask someone to point her out…. Have fun, precious."

The matter settled in her own pigheaded mind, at least, Samantha hung up before Lucas could summon up another argument.

Although there were those who might argue the point, Lucas had always considered himself a levelheaded man. He did not believe in ghosts, vampires, aliens or Bigfoot. He considered the Loch Ness monster an ingenious tourism ploy, hadn't had any reason to think about the Tooth Fairy since he'd lost his last baby molar during a scuffle on the baseball field two weeks before his eleventh birthday, and the jury was still out on the existence of his guardian angel.

However, as he walked into the gilded lobby of the San Francisco Whitfield Palace Hotel, Lucas decided he must have somehow passed through a curtain in time and space. Or else he'd gotten some bad pepperoni on the pizza he'd had for lunch today.

Women dressed in hoopskirts the diameter of the Liberty Bell were gathered in small groups, chatting pleasantly with kohl-eyed vampires, Stetson-clad cowgirls, Pocahontas look-alikes and at least two women dressed in what appeared to be filmy white nightgowns with huge, white-feathered wings extending from the back of their shoulders. Those feathers, combined with all the female voices chirping at the same time, gave him the feeling of walking into an aviary on some alien planet.

He checked in at the desk, requesting a room next to Roberta Grace. Fortunately, the agency put most of their out-of-town clients in the hotel, which gave him clout. Although it took a bit of finagling and some fast talking, adjoining rooms were arranged. After being assured by the manager that the bell captain would have his garment bag taken upstairs to his room, Lucas went in search of Roberta Grace.

He was still trying to decide whether to escape while he had the chance, or attempt to wade through the feminine throng to the oyster bar, when a woman leaped out from behind a marble pillar and grabbed his arm. She was wearing a low-cut, blue silk gown, a towering powdered wig and enough fake jewelry to ensure death by drowning if she were unfortunate enough to trip into the lobby fountain.

"Thank heavens! Where on earth have you been?"

"In Sausalito." Lucas decided that if this was the woman he'd come here to meet, the deal was off.

"You were supposed to be here ages ago."

"Hey, I figured if I was going to have to work this shindig, you'd want me to take time to pick up the appropriate clothes."

She was looking at him as if *he* were the strange one. "That doesn't explain why you weren't here as promised. Two hours ago."

The badge pinned to her breast revealed her to be Marianne Tyler, a member of the conference coordinating committee. There were enough multicolored ribbons attached to the badge to suggest she'd just won Best of Show.

"Look, I think we must have our wires crossed here—"

"I'll say we do!" The furrows in her brow deepened. "If you think I'm paying your entire agency fee, when you're so horrendously late, you can think again, young man. And you're not in costume." She eyed him with frustration. "Where's your cutlass? Your agent promised you'd have a cutlass."

"I'm sorry, ma'am. But I don't have any idea what you're talking about."

"You're not my pirate?"

"No, ma'am. I'm not."

"Oh." Her lips drew into a tight line as she gave him a long silent perusal from the top of his dark head down to his boots. Then back up again. "It was probably your hair that threw me off," she decided. "Most normal men are wearing it short these days."

Lucas wasn't about to get into a discussion about normalcy with a woman who appeared to take fashion tips from Marie Antoinette. "That and the fact that I seem to be the only man in the hotel," he suggested helpfully.

"Women are always in the majority at these things. Which is why a good-looking male is such a draw." She continued to gaze up at him. "You know," she said speculatively, "since my pirate still hasn't shown up, perhaps you'd like to fill in."

Lucas had been shot at on more than one occasion. He'd fought hand-to-hand for his life in a South American jungle while nearly delirious with malaria. In his former life as a SEAL, he'd swam from a bone-chilling sea onto a distant shore on a moonless night with a knife between his teeth prepared for the worst. But the speculative gleam in this woman's pale blue eyes was the most frightening thing he'd ever witnessed.

"Now there's an idea," he drawled. "But I'm afraid, since I have a previous engagement, I'm going to have to decline."

"Oh, dear. And you would have been so perfect. The ladies would have gone wild for that scar on your cheek. It makes you look *très* dashing." When she shook her head with regret, pins flew out of the snowy white beehive onto the plush red-and-gold carpeting. "Well, I suppose I have no choice but to keep looking. He has to be here somewhere."

With that the conference coordinating committee woman took off with a rustle of silk.

Hell. If he hadn't stopped to clean out his desk, he'd already be headed for blue seas. As he continued to make his way through the crowds of women, Lucas wished he'd never answered that damn phone in the first place.

Neptune's Table was, unsurprisingly, as packed as the lobby. He stood in the doorway, looking past the iced trays of raw oysters lined up on the half shell, scanning the tables of women, searching out someone who might fit Samantha's sketchy description.

He found her on the second survey of the room, sitting alone, half-hidden beneath a towering banana palm. Unlike most of the patrons, who were dressed in evening clothes or elaborate costumes, she was wearing a silk suit the color of sunshine on wheat, with an ivory blouse buttoned all the way to the throat and fastened with a cameo. Also, unlike the other patrons, she was working. Her fingers were literally racing over the slate gray keyboard of the laptop computer, and her eyes, behind a pair of tortoiseshell glasses, were intensely focused on the screen.

Lucas crossed the room to her table. Lost in her writing, she remained oblivious to him. He cleared his throat. Nothing. Just a frown as she backspaced furiously, erasing the words on the screen. He tried again. "Excuse me?"

Murmuring something that could have been a curse, she looked up at him. As their eyes met, then momentarily held, Lucas imagined the roar of distant surf and felt himself drowning. And the crazy thing about it was that he didn't even care.

"If I'm wrong, this is going to sound like the world's worst pickup line. But are you the lady I'm supposed to spend the weekend with?"

She surprised him by blushing, pink color flooding prettily into cheeks so creamy she could have been the poster girl for milk. He wouldn't have expected a woman who penned steamy romance novels to be shy. But damned if she didn't seem to be.

"I wouldn't exactly put it that way."

"But you are Roberta Grace?"

"Actually, I'm Grace Fairfield. Roberta Grace is my pseudonym. And you must be Lucas Kincaid."

"That's me." He held out his hand.

After a moment's hesitation, she held out her own. Her short, neat nails were unlacquered, and a silver band, fashioned into interwoven Celtic knots, adorned her ring finger. Her skin was buttery smooth, cool and fragrant.

"I have a friend who reads romance novels." Recognition clicked as Lucas envisioned this woman's name penned in fancy gold script across the front of a book cover. "She was reading one of yours last week, now that I think about it. Bodice rippers, right?"

Grace Fairfield lifted her chin. Repressed passions swirled intriguingly in her eyes, contrasting with the earlier shyness. Lucas had always been a man who appreciated contrasts. He was also discovering that he was a sucker for a female in glasses.

"That just happens to be an outdated and inaccurate, not to mention insulting, term, Mr. Kincaid. For the record, I've never ripped a bodice yet."

"Neither have I," Lucas said easily. Enjoying her hauteur the same way he was enjoying looking at her, he pulled up a wooden chair and sat down at the small round table. He couldn't quite decide whether her eyes were green or blue. But they sure were pretty. "But hope springs eternal."

When she didn't laugh, as he'd intended, or so much as crack a smile, he decided to try again. "I'm sorry. I certainly didn't mean to insult you, Ms. Fairfield." He pulled a contrition-laced smile from his repertoire, one that had always worked wonders with women from Seattle to Singapore.

The corners of her lips tilted. Just barely, but enough to let him know he was off the hook. For now.

"Apology accepted. And I didn't mean to sound huffy. It's just that you hit a sensitive spot."

"I understand." The idea of searching out a few more of the lady's sensitive spots was definitely appealing. Samantha had been wrong about Grace's hair. Mousy? It was the color of the melted caramel his mother used to dip apples in every fall. It was also as shiny as a shampoo commercial and looked as if it'd be soft to the touch. Lucas allowed himself a brief fantasy of loosening it from that tidy little knot she'd fashioned it into at the nape of her neck. "I also didn't mean to interrupt your work."

"That's all right." She hit the keys, saving the text. "I was going to have to be stopping soon, anyway. I'm scheduled to judge the costume pageant at tonight's welcoming party."

"Ah." He nodded. "That explains the belly dancer." He tilted his head in the direction of a woman clad in spangles and purple chiffon who was drinking a Bloody Mary and downing raw oysters with three more women all dressed like Dr. Quinn, Medicine Woman.

"The conference operates on several levels," she explained. "Some of the attendees come here to network. Others to visit with friends, some to gain writing tips and publisher information from the seminars. But since just about everyone also enjoys a party, there are times it can seem a bit like a three-ring circus."

He tipped the wooden chair on its back legs and grinned at her. "Lucky for me that I've always enjoyed circuses."

She took off the dark-framed reading glasses and studied him. The frown that replaced the faint smile was not encouraging.

"So, I guess you're in need of a hero?" he asked.

"No." When she bit her bottom lip, Lucas decided that the sight of those white teeth sinking into that soft pink flesh was about the sexiest damn thing he'd ever seen. "I mean, I don't think so, and I'm certain I'm overreacting. But I received another letter when I arrived at the hotel this morning, and…" Her voice drifted off.

"Yeah, my boss told me about the letters. She said something about them threatening you?"

"Well, yes." Grace felt the embarrassed color flood into her cheeks and wished she'd just continued to ignore them. After all, Tina was undoubtedly right. Who would want to kill her? The idea was ludicrous. "I suppose," she said reluctantly, "you could call them death threats."

He glanced around the room. "Well, you've definitely landed in one helluva pool of suspects."

Her remarkable eyes widened. "Oh, I can't believe any one of my friends would be capable of writing such letters. We're a very close group," she insisted.

Lucas suspected the Borgias had probably said the same thing on occasion. "Perhaps you should let me see them," he suggested.

"Oh. Of course." She'd gone from pretty pink to paper pale, and although he had to give her credit for making a good stab at appearing composed, Lucas didn't miss the tremor of her hand as she reached into her purse and took out the envelopes.

Deciding that they'd already lost the chance to check for fingerprints, he took them from her, noticing that the postmarks were from four different cities in three different states.

The paper and envelopes could have been purchased from any office supply store in the country. From the justified margins, he knew they'd been written on a computer, which made him wish for the good old days when a detective could track down a culprit by the idiosyncracies of a typewriter—a raised *e*, perhaps, or a broken crossbar on a *t*. He turned his attention to the rambling, often incoherent prose.

Grace watched him read the letters that had caused her so many sleepless nights, and admired his absolute concentration. She imagined a bomb could go off in the middle of the bar and he wouldn't even notice. She knew the feeling well, since she was the same way herself, whenever she was writing. The thought that she and this hero-for-hire could have anything in common was more than a little disconcerting.

His dark hair, pulled back into a very unbusinesslike ponytail, could have appeared artistic on another man, but instead gave him a rakish, dangerous appearance. When her nerves tangled again, Grace assured herself that she could handle them. After all, she certainly had in far worse situations.

After he'd read each letter carefully and twice, Lucas lifted his head. His gaze collided with hers. The air in the bar was suddenly electric, like heat lightning shimmering on a distant horizon.

Lucas had always enjoyed women. He liked the way they felt—like the undersides of the snowy blossoms on his grandmother Fancy's blue ribbon–winning camellias. He liked the way they smelled; liked the smooth, enticing, catlike way they moved; liked the way they tasted. The truth was, he flat-out loved everything about the opposite sex, and since women sensed that, mostly they liked him right back. Which had always suited him just fine.

He'd settled down a lot since his younger days, when he'd felt almost honor bound to live up to the old naval tradition of a girl in every port. But even so, he'd always enjoyed playing the field too much to narrow it down to a single woman.

Until now.

Her lips were full and pink and shiny from being licked. From nerves, Lucas guessed. Lord help him, he wanted to taste them. Actually, he wanted to taste the rest of her, too. Every lush, perfumed inch.

A little pool of silence settled over them.

Grace was the first to break it. "So," she said, a bit breathlessly. "Do you think I'm in danger?"

They both were, Lucas thought. And suspected there wasn't a thing either one of them could do about it. Fate, he decided, had one helluva quirky sense of humor.

"It's obvious that whoever wrote them is a card-carrying paranoiac." The letters professed a belief that Roberta Grace was spying on the letter writer and then stealing the writer's real-life adventures to use in the Roberta Grace books. "I'd say it's a distinct possibility."

He rubbed his chin and vaguely wished he'd taken time to shave before driving back into the city. "Is there an outside chance that you could have accidentally written about some true instances in someone's life?"

"That would be extremely difficult, since my books are set in eras ranging from medieval France to nineteenth-century Arizona."

"Well, that definitely narrows our suspect list," Lucas decided.

"Oh? Why's that?"

"It's obvious that we're dealing with a time traveler. So all we have to do is keep an eye out for the Way-Back Machine, and it should be a cinch to keep you safe."

This time her smile was quick and warm and genuine. The thickly lashed eyes he knew he was going to be dreaming about tonight brightened.

"And to think people no longer believe in truth in advertising," she murmured, wondering what the chances were of actually finding a genuine hero in the classifieds. She wasn't certain that even she would get away with such a plot.

"We've never lost a client yet." As he watched those ripe, petal pink lips curve in a faint smile, Lucas reminded himself that he'd never stooped to begging for anything in his life. And he wasn't going to start now. Even if Grace Fairfield was the type of woman who made a man want to run out and buy some long-stemmed red roses and a gilt box of rich, melt-in-the-mouth chocolates.

"So," he said, dragging this thoughts back to his reason for being at the hotel in the first place, "why don't you tell me the names of all the people you think might have it in for you?"

"Oh, I can't believe it could be anyone I know," she said quickly. Too quickly. She fell silent and dragged her gaze over to the tropical fish tank along the far wall. Although patience had never been his long suit, Lucas waited her out.

"I suppose Robert might qualify."

"Robert?" The pieces instantly fell into place. "That'd be the other half of Roberta Grace?"

"That's right. Robert Radcliffe is my former husband."

Lucas made a mental note to check out Radcliffe ASAP.

Any guy stupid enough to let this woman get away had to have more than a few screws loose. Enough to threaten murder? Lucas wondered. "So you two collaborated?"

"That's what Robert has always told people."

"Why do I hear a 'but' in that?"

"I have no idea." She folded her arms across the front of her suit jacket. "You have to understand, Mr. Kincaid, that Robert is not exactly my favorite subject. Our divorce was, unfortunately, not without its unpleasant moments." From the flame that flashed in her eyes, Lucas decided that was an understatement.

"And you have to understand, Ms. Fairfield, that if you want me to protect your life, we're not going to be able to ignore past unpleasant moments. Since they tend to be the ones that lead to murder."

"Point taken," she said quietly. Grace rubbed at her temples, where a headache threatened. *Murder.* It was such an ugly word. She still couldn't believe it.

"Have you called the police about these letters?"

"No. I'm a very private person. Besides, in the beginning Tina and I decided that they were merely some unstable reader letting off emotional steam."

"And Tina would be…?"

"My agent, Tina Parker." Who definitely wouldn't be all that thrilled to discover her client had hired a bodyguard, Grace feared, but did not say. "Although I'll admit to being uneasy about the letters, I agreed with her that there's no point in creating headlines. After all, I've had enough negative publicity lately, what with the divorce, and the lawsuit—"

"Lawsuit?" Lucas hated going into a job without sufficient background.

Grace sighed. Talking about Robert was her least favorite thing to do. Even below root canals and swimsuit shopping. Deciding her bodyguard would hear the gossip anyway, Grace decided it was better if it come directly from her.

"Robert is suing me for the rights to the Roberta Grace name." She lifted her chin in the same challenging way she'd done when Lucas had inadvertently insulted her books. "My novels are my sole intellectual property. I have no intention of relinquishing a name I've worked very hard to establish to a man who never wrote a single publishable sentence."

There. She'd finally said it out loud. Grace wondered how she could have been so stupid to go along with the so-called collaboration lie in the first place.

"Makes sense to me." Money was a popular motive for murder. Strike two against the ex-husband, Lucas decided.

"So, what about Tina? Did she continue to represent your ex?"

"No. He has a new agent now. Actually, it's our former editor."

There was a lot more there, Lucas determined. A lot more Grace was going to have to tell him, no matter how upsetting it proved. After all, wounded pride was a lot less painful than murder.

2

GRACE BRACED HERSELF for Lucas to ask for details about her divorce. She was also surprised that he hadn't seen the stories that had taunted her for months whenever she'd been forced to wait in a supermarket line.

She'd gotten so accustomed to public humiliation that it hadn't occurred to her that there'd actually be anyone left on the planet that hadn't heard of her. Or read about her messy divorce, which had encouraged even the so-called establishment press to stoop to purple prose in their reporting. She couldn't bear to think what would happen if the news of her threatening letters got out.

"There's one thing I have to insist upon, if I hire you," she said.

Lucas decided it was a moot point to mention that he was accustomed to being the one who'd choose whether or not he'd take a case. "Shoot."

"I'd need you to be discreet. It's been a horrendous year for me, both privately and professionally, and I'm in contract negotiations with a new management team. The last thing I need is for such an unsavory story to hit the tabloids."

"Actually," he corrected mildly, "the last thing you need is for some nutcase to try to make good on those threats."

His words caused ice to skim up her spine. She honestly hadn't expected him to take the letters seriously. In fact, her main reason for having called the 800 number she'd seen in a newspaper this morning while flying out West was to have a security expert officially declare them harmless.

After all, she received all sorts of strange mail—some from prisoners, including an unsavory man on death row who, for some obscure reason Grace would never understand, claimed to identify with her heroes.

And then there'd been the ten-page letter scribbled on filler paper from someone alleging to have been in an outer-space harem with Grace. Supposedly, they'd both been beamed aboard a spaceship and taken to a woman-less planet of sex-starved males who inexplicably resembled Tommy Lee Jones from the movie *Men in Black*. At the time, Grace had figured she should be so lucky.

"I still can't believe the threats are legitimate," she murmured, as if saying the words out loud could make them true.

Before Lucas could answer Grace's latest denial, a woman in a red knit power suit and very high heels stopped beside the table.

"There you are!" she exclaimed to Grace. "I've been searching everywhere for you. Alice Vail insists on speaking with you before the costume pageant and—"

"Who's Alice Vail?" Lucas asked, breaking in.

She shot him an impatient look. "A reviewer for one of the romance-genre fan magazines." Both her attitude and her voice were New York brisk. Her hair had been cut in an ultrashort, trendy style, and her lips, which were drawn into a suspicious line, had been painted the same scarlet as her suit. "She's always been a supporter of romance novels, and consistently gives Roberta Grace rave reviews...and who are you?"

"Lucas Kincaid," he answered, excusing her rudeness, since she was obviously a Yankee. "I'm—"

"An old friend." Grace cut in quickly. She covered his

hand with hers, linking their fingers together as she smiled at him across the table. "From college." Her fingers tightened in silent warning; her expressive eyes pleaded with him to go along with her, then looked back at the woman. "This is Tina Parker, my agent. You've no idea what a surprise it was to discover Lucas was living here in San Francisco."

"It was sure a surprise to pick up my morning paper and read that my old college sweetheart was going to be visiting our fair city." He skimmed a fingertip down the back of her hand, rewarded when he felt the trail of warmth bloom beneath his touch.

"College sweetheart?" the agent asked with obvious suspicion. She turned back to Grace. "I thought Robert the Rat was your college sweetheart."

"He was my college mistake," Grace corrected.

"Grace and I had a fight," Lucas improvised. "One of those little foolish spats young lovers have." He gave Grace a warm look rife with what appeared to be honest regret. "The funny thing is that I can't even remember what it was about. Can you, darlin'?"

"No," Grace managed to answer, her voice weaker than she would have wished. *His* baritone voice had deepened, the rich Dixie drawl reminding Grace of a steamy summer research trip she'd taken two years ago to Savannah. It brought back warm memories of gracious pillared antebellum homes, frosty glasses of mint-sprigged iced tea and deep-fried food that had added inches to her hips even as it pleasured her taste buds. Unfortunately, a foolish, romantic part of her was finding Lucas Kincaid every bit as tempting. "I can't."

"I suppose it doesn't matter." He sighed and looked up at the still-skeptical agent. "The short sad story is that she slept with the rat to make me jealous, and the next thing I knew they were working on her book together—the one I always knew was going to be a blockbuster hit."

"*Ransomed Hearts*," Tina Parker murmured.

"That's it. Dynamite story. And based on our own romance, of course."

"Oh?"

"She never told you?"

"Told me what?"

Lucas shook his head with mock regret, stood up and pulled up a chair for her. "You may as well sit down. This could take awhile."

She actually looked tempted. Then, as if remembering her mission, she gazed pointedly down at her watch. "You're scheduled to judge the costume pageant in less than two hours," she reminded Grace. "And Alice doesn't like to be kept waiting."

Grace had never been comfortable with interviews. Which was why Robert, who loved the spotlight, had always volunteered to handle them. Unfortunately, he'd also used the opportunity to let people believe that he was actually the creative force behind the bestselling Roberta Grace books.

Deciding that the reviewer was obviously the best person to set the record straight, Grace rose. "Where is she?"

"In the concierge lounge. I suggested we meet in your suite, but the officious little man at the front desk informed me that there'd been a mixup."

"Robert somehow ended up in the presidential suite. The substitute room they assigned me isn't ready yet."

"I can't believe this!" An exasperated breath puffed from between Tina's pursed crimson lips. "Did you explain who you were?"

"Of course. But when I agreed to give the keynote address, the conference committee naturally reserved the room in the name of Roberta Grace."

"And the Rat got it first." A hatred Lucas didn't think was feigned glittered in the agent's eyes. She looked up at him the same way the harried woman in the lobby had—as if casting him for a part in her own personal movie. "You never said what you did for a living. I don't suppose you'd happen to be a hit man?"

"No, ma'am." At least, not any longer. "I'm sorry."

"So am I. It was such a lovely idea." She gave him another considering look. "What *do* you do, by the way?"

"I design computer software." That much, at least, was the truth.

"Ah." Lucas could practically see the wheels clicking away in her head. "Computer books can be big sellers. Do you have an agent?"

"No, but—"

"Here." She took a gray pasteboard card from her alligator bag and handed it to him. "I have my own agency in New York and represent some of the top names in publishing. Will you be available for a little private chat sometime during the next few days?"

"Absolutely."

Although it wasn't technically his job to find the person writing the threatening letters, in order to protect Grace, Lucas had to know the players. Which meant he intended to speak with all the suspects. And although he couldn't think of any reason why an agent would want to kill a client who undoubtedly represented a hefty percentage of her yearly income, he wasn't about to disregard anyone.

"I'm not about to run off now that I've found my girl again after all these years." The smile he flashed at Tina was as rakish as any high seas buccaneer. "I'll be staying at the hotel for the entire conference. With Gracie."

"Well." Once again he admired the mental gymnastics as he watched the agent consider the various publicity aspects of this announcement. "Isn't that nice? And how timely that Grace's current book, *This Time Forever*, is about reunited lovers." Obviously, she'd decided this happy coincidence was beneficial to her client's career. "Make certain you tell Alice all about your second chance at love, Grace."

Grace could tell that Tina was already writing the headlines for the press releases. "You know I'm uncomfortable discussing my personal life."

"I know your personal life has been thrown all over the tabloids lately," Tina countered. "You should be grateful for an opportunity to get some good press for a change." She shot a mock glare a long, long way up at Lucas. "You'd better treat her well, Lucas Kincaid. Or you'll have me to answer to."

"Yes, ma'am." Ignoring the way Grace stiffened, he brushed his lips against the top of her head. Across the bar at least one camera flashed. "Let's go, darlin'. You don't want to keep your fans waiting."

"You've nothing to worry about, Grace." Tina's smile offered reassurance. "Alice has always loved your books. And you're so much more likable than Robert. You're going to be dynamite at promotion."

Personally, Grace didn't believe that last part. But since she wasn't about to argue in public, she murmured what could have been an agreement and left the bar, Lucas close beside her, his hand on her back.

"And for the record, Alice Vail is not a fan," Grace muttered as they made their way across the lobby. She moved away, breaking the light contact that was warming her skin beneath her suit. "She's a reviewer. There's a difference."

Irritation was radiating off her in shimmering waves as she made a beeline for the bank of elevators. Having a pretty good idea what she was upset about, Lucas didn't push for conversation.

Surprisingly, given the number of women already congregated in the lobby, the elevator was empty. They stood side by side, each watching the numbers flash above the door.

"You're angry," Lucas said after they'd passed the fourth floor.

"You had no right to tell Tina that lie about us having been lovers."

"You didn't seem to want her to know I was a bodyguard."

"Well, that's true, but—"

"And she probably wouldn't have believed I was trying to sell you life insurance."

"No. Especially since I already have a very hefty policy."

They'd now passed the fifth floor. "Let me guess. The divorce settlement requires you to keep making payments on your life insurance policy."

"If I die, as beneficiary, Robert gets everything," she revealed glumly. It was not a pretty thought. Especially after she'd foolishly given Robert the Rat so many years of her life. Not to mention royalties.

"Well, then, I guess we'll just have to keep you alive." A man comfortable with touching, he idly tucked an escaped strand of caramel hair behind her ear.

"The ad in the paper said your agency has an admirable success rate."

"We do."

They exchanged a long look that had that pretty color tingeing her cheeks again and made Lucas want to press the Stop button so he could kiss her for a very long time.

"I wish we'd had time to talk about how we're going to explain you being here at the conference," she murmured. "While I certainly don't want you hovering over me like some kind of overprotective guard dog, I'm not certain that letting people think you're an old lover is such a good idea, either."

One thing Lucas had always hated about this bodyguard gig was when clients made things difficult by insisting that he pretend to be something he wasn't. However, this time the idea of playing lover to Grace Fairfield suited him just fine.

The elevator had glass walls, allowing a view of the bay, where blue waters lured Lucas to freedom. But Grace's siren song was proving even more enticing.

She smelled of spring—of green leaves, soft rains and jonquils. The slanting rays of afternoon sun streaming through the tinted windows streaked her caramel hair with honey, and her voluptuous body was definitely a pleasing change from all the stick-thin city women he was accustomed to seeing in San Francisco.

If he'd been in the market for a figurehead for his boat, Lucas would have wanted this woman to pose for it. If he'd been looking for a woman to have his children, he would have ended his search right here and now.

His gaze drifted to her magnificent breasts, making him wonder what, exactly, she was wearing under that wheat-hued suit and primly buttoned silk blouse. Having already caught a glimpse of hidden passions flowing beneath her smooth, controlled surface, he suspected satin and lace.

"Everyone loves reunion stories," he reminded her. "If nothing else, it should drive your ex a little nuts to know that you're moving on. Instead of sitting around bemoaning your failed marriage."

She didn't answer immediately, just gave him a long, slow perusal in a way that made him wonder if she was comparing him to her fictionalized romantic heroes. And if so, how he fared in the competition.

"Robert's ego will implode if he thinks we're sleeping

together," she murmured, more to herself than to him. "And as petty as that undoubtedly makes me, I rather like the idea."

She wasn't the only one.

Oh yes, Lucas thought with masculine anticipation, watching over this woman's body wouldn't prove any hardship. He could spare a few days. After all, Alaska wasn't going anywhere.

The private lounge assigned to guests staying on the concierge level of the hotel boasted dazzling vistas of the city. But Lucas guessed none of the individuals in the room had even bothered to glance out the floor-to-ceiling windows at the world-famous view. A blond pianist in a long black dress was playing a pretty fair Gershwin on a jet black Steinway, but no one seemed to be listening, either. Romance might be the means by which these women earned their living, but there was nothing romantic about the aura of business mingling in the air with the expensive perfumes. During his past eighteen months working as a bodyguard for S. J. Slade, he'd been in Fortune 500 boardrooms that hadn't exuded such energy.

Lucas had always possessed a strong intuitive sense; during his days as a SEAL his life had often depended on it. And right now, every instinct he possessed told him that although Grace was doing an admirable job of hiding it, she was more than a little nervous as they waded across the carpeting to where a seventy-something woman dressed in a white lace blouse and flowing multi-hued gypsy skirt was holding court. Her hair, a bright flame color that did not appear in nature, was piled high on her head, the beehive resembling a bobbin on an industrial sewing machine.

"You remind me of a woman on the way to the guillotine," he murmured.

"At least beheading's over quickly," Grace murmured

back. "They put a black bag over your head, you kneel down and swoosh, it's over before you can make it through a Hail Mary."

She paused and turned toward him. "How do I look?"

Since she'd asked, Lucas allowed himself a masculine study. Her blue-green hazel eyes, which in this light appeared almost turquoise, were both intelligent and expressive. Her face was too pale, almost translucent, like the fine bone china his mother brought out only for Thanksgiving, Christmas and other special occasions.

As for her body... "Absolutely stunning."

He watched the color drift into her face again, like wild strawberries on a field of snow, and surprised himself by being drawn to a woman capable of blushing in this modern age.

His voice was too deep. Too husky. Too male. Although Grace was used to being at eye level with most men, this man topped her with several inches to spare. And the way he was looking down at her, as if he were a chocoholic and she was a Hershey bar, caused a fluttering in her stomach.

"That wasn't what I was talking about." Because she had a sudden urge to reach up and touch his dark cheek, to skim her fingertips along that intriguing white crescent, she folded her hands tightly together. "My hair," she asked, remembering the casual, confident way he'd tucked the loose strand behind her ear, "is it—"

"Perfect."

"My lipstick—"

"Perfect." Deciding that since he'd technically resigned, it wouldn't be unprofessional to touch, just a bit, he took his hands from the security of his pockets and ran his palms over her shoulders in a gesture meant to soothe her and please himself.

"Everything about you is absolutely perfect." The con-

versational buzz in the room dwindled away, replaced by
a rapt silence as every female eye in the lounge focused on
them. "If you'd like me to go into detail—"

"No." Grace was unnerved by the strange little kick in
her heart. His hands were wide and strong. But gentle.
They were also too appealing for comfort. She'd sworn,
after the debacle with Robert, that the only males in her
life would be the ones in her books. Wanting to back
away, but all too aware that they were the center of un-
wanted attention, she held her ground. And stiffened her
spine. "That's not necessary."

"Maybe later."

His rakish smile was both charming and dangerous.
She stared, momentarily entranced by the dimple that
flashed right below the thin white scar, then took a brief
moment to level her nerves and her voice.

"Maybe not."

That said, she managed, just barely, to keep her head
high while she walked away on legs that felt like limp
spaghetti.

Enjoying her flare of independent spirit, Lucas chuckled as he followed her across the lounge to where Alice
Vail was seated in a high-backed gilt chair vaguely remi-
niscent of a throne.

"Hello, Alice," Grace greeted the reviewer with a warm
smile designed to conceal her nerves. She bent, bestowing
a kiss to the powdered cheek. "It's lovely to see you
again."

"Good to see you, too, dear." The clever eyes took a
quick judicious perusal. "You're looking very well. All
things considered."

"I'm feeling well," Grace said, not quite truthfully. "All
things considered."

"It's lovely that you've decided to come out of seclu-
sion. You've been missed." She lifted a pair of rhinestone-

framed butterfly glasses on a pearl chain from her bosom and zeroed in on Lucas. "Are you, by any chance, the pirate Marianne's been searching the hotel for?"

"No, ma'am," he answered politely, thinking there was definitely something to be said for getting his hair chopped off into a military buzz cut before this conference was over.

"You could be. Which means, I suppose, you're another entrant for tonight's cover-model contest?" She gave him a longer look. "While you admittedly possess a certain natural machismo that's head and shoulders above most of the ones I've seen, I'm afraid looks alone aren't going to be enough to win the grand prize."

She chewed thoughtfully on a fingernail painted the deep violet of pansies. "Although you're a natural for the pirate, they've been horribly overdone lately." She skimmed her gaze down him. "How are your legs?"

Lucas exchanged a quick glance with Grace and noticed that for someone who'd been so damn nervous only a minute earlier, she certainly seemed to be enjoying herself at his expense. "My legs?"

"If they're halfway decent and not too hairy, you'd look stunning in a kilt. And, of course, with Scotland so popular right now, you'd be a shoo-in to win." Dangling gold earrings shaped like old-fashioned plumed pens bounced as she nodded, satisfied. "Yes, definitely a kilt."

"Lucas isn't a cover model." Grace knew it was a bit petty of her, but she was actually enjoying his obvious discomfort at being taken for a male model. It had been a very long time since she'd found humor in anything.

"Then what, and who, is he?" A penciled, bright brow arched above the rhinestone-studded frames. "Obviously you're a brave man, whoever you are. Daring to breach this coven of females."

"I was thinking exactly the same thing when I first arrived." This one would have been a firecracker in her day, Lucas thought. "I'm Lucas Kincaid, Miz Vail. And Grace and I are old friends. From college."

"Really?" She took a delicate, gold-rim cup bearing the world-famous crown logo of the hotel from the spindly-legged table beside her chair and sipped thoughtfully as she considered that idea. "Isn't that interesting?" She turned back to Grace. "I'd thought Robert was your college beau."

"I was the guy she dumped for the Rat," Lucas explained.

Alice Vail gave him a longer, more in-depth perusal from head to toe. "Gracious. And here I'd always considered Grace to be an intelligent young woman."

"It's a long story." Grace broke in, shooting Lucas another dark, warning look. "And I know how pressed for time you are, Alice."

"Oh, I'm never to busy to talk with one of my favorite writers. And her friends. Especially the drop-dead-gorgeous male ones." She looked up at Lucas through a set of thick, double false lashes. "You've certainly chosen a dashing escort for your return to public life, Grace, dear.

"If I were thirty years younger, Mr. Kincaid, I do believe I'd give our dear Grace a little competition."

"If my daddy hadn't taught me that it wasn't gentlemanly to step out on a lady you're courting, I'd certainly welcome it, Miz Vail."

"Flatterer." She fluttered an imaginary fan. "My third—and favorite—husband was a southern gentleman." Grace stared as the maven of romance reviews, the woman who could, on occasion, make grown writers quake in their high heels, simpered like a Southern belle. "From Savannah."

"Well now, that practically made us neighbors. I'm

from Raintree, Georgia." Grace noticed that Lucas's drawl had gotten thick enough to pour on pancakes.

"Ah. Lovely little town. Or so I've heard."

"I've always thought so. Nice, friendly folks, too."

"So William always said. We weren't married long enough for me to actually discover your Southern hospitality for myself—William harbored an unfortunate attraction to Tennessee whiskey and showgirls—but I've always thought I might visit someday."

"Just let me know when. Though I travel a lot, I'll make a point of coming home to give you the grand tour."

"Be careful, young man." She tapped a silver-tipped cane on the carpet. "I may just take you up on that offer." Warning given, she turned back toward Grace. "Mr. Kincaid is a decided improvement over that scoundrel Robert. Who is, by the way, going to be chewing nails when he catches sight of you two."

"It's been quite a few years since college," Grace reminded her. "Lucas and I are merely friends now."

"Of course, dear," Alice replied in a tone that suggested she didn't believe a word. "I hate to even bring up your errant spouse while we're having such a lovely chat, but have you seen him yet?"

"No."

Although Grace would dearly love to give Robert hell for having stolen her suite, there was another, strong part of her that wished she could go the entire conference without running into Robert the Rat. Unfortunately, since the last book they'd "collaborated" on was a finalist for a ROMI, the romance industry's award for excellence, she was expected to sit at the publisher's table with her former husband at Saturday night's awards banquet.

"I had the misfortune to speak with the scoundrel earlier," Alice revealed. "He was with his new agent. Your former editor," she tacked on scathingly. "I must say, they certainly didn't behave much like honeymooners. There was definitely a negative tension between them."

That little revelation about the former editor becoming the Rat's new wife caught Lucas's instant attention. Obviously Grace hadn't been kidding when she'd mentioned that the divorce had been far from cordial.

"The odious little man actually had the gall to interrupt my tête-à-tête with Patricia Gardner Evans to inform me that he's going to be writing the next book in the Scarlett O'Hara saga," Alice continued, obviously enjoying being the one to pass this tidbit on.

"Personally, I've always believed Margaret Mitchell knew exactly when to end that story," Grace said.

"Ha!" There was another sharp, satisfied tap of the cane. "That's precisely what I told Robert. I also did a little checking after he'd slunk away, and the contractual matters are far from settled, of course.

"The family, as well as the publisher, are insisting on a very detailed synopsis and several sample chapters. It was my impression that they have far less confidence in his ability to pull off a story now that you two aren't collaborating."

Grace wished she could be a fly on the wall when the editors got their first look at those chapters. For whatever you wanted to say about the spouse-stealing Buffy Cunningham Radcliffe, she'd been an excellent editor. But she was no miracle worker. It would undoubtedly be easier to spin gold from straw than to turn Robert's wooden prose into anything remotely publishable.

"Well, as much as I've adored visiting with you, Alice, I really must dash. I'm due to judge the costume competition this evening and I still have to change."

"It's been lovely seeing you, dear. And I'm sure we'll run into each other again before the weekend is over. And of course, I'll be pleased to toast your success at the celebration party the magazine is putting on for the ROMI winners after the awards banquet Saturday night.

"Oh, and by the way, I've given you a five-platinum-hearts review for *Destiny's Darling*. It was, without a doubt, the best western historical romance I've read in years."

"Thank you." Grace had thought her upcoming book, the first without Robert's name on the copyright, the novel that had been literally wrenched out of her during the painful divorce process, had been her best work yet. She'd hoped reviewers—and more importantly, the readers—would agree. Of course, in a way, she'd been fortunate; Robert had, after all, provided a great deal of grist for her creative mill.

"I especially enjoyed the character of the snake oil salesman," Alice said. "He was such a treacherous devil, peddling those phony cures to the sick and desperate. Why, when he began gunrunning and selling bootleg whiskey to the Indians, I swear my blood actually began to boil. And when he struck his wife... Well, let's just say that having the Apaches stake him out in the boiling, Arizona-desert sun was brilliant revenge."

"I'm delighted you enjoyed it." Since Robert had been the inspiration for her slimiest villain ever, Grace had certainly enjoyed the vengeance fantasy.

"Immensely. However, everyone knows I can be horribly bloodthirsty."

Knowing how the strong-minded woman's reviews could, on occasion, draw blood, Grace didn't comment.

3

"A KILT?" Luke murmured as they walked away.

"Just be grateful she didn't order you to roll up your pant legs so she could take a look. Or worse yet, pull down your jeans so she could check out how you'd look in a loin cloth." A mental image of Lucas clad in a brief piece of buckskin caused Grace's unruly hormones to spike.

"Now there's a thought." The hotel staff had set up the happy hour buffet. Lucas watched as a clutch of female vampires and another Marie Antoinette look-alike began filling up plates.

"Actually," Grace admitted, "although I hate to pump up your male ego any more than it's undoubtedly already been inflated since you arrived, you'd certainly look better than some of the models I've had on my covers."

"Why, thank you, darlin'." He grinned down at her and tugged on another silky strand of hair that had escaped confinement to curl over her milkmaid's cheek. "That's exactly what you were supposed to say." Ignoring the way she backed away from him, he glanced over at the buffet. "Want to grab a bite before the festivities?"

Grace's nerves had been too on edge to eat all day. Now, strangely, with Lucas at her side, although she was much too aware of him as a male, she realized she was starving.

"Just a bite." She still had her gown to get into for the dinner cruise tomorrow evening, and with all the food that was always served at RNN conferences, if she wasn't careful, she'd have to hire heavy machinery to hook her into her strapless long-line bra.

Deciding she'd just have to get used to him touching her, since he fully intended to do a lot more of it, Lucas put his hand on Grace's waist and deftly led her through the throng to a table in the corner. "Wait here. I'll get you a plate."

"I'm more than capable of feeding myself, Mr. Kincaid."

"Well, of course you are, Ms. Fairfield. But one of us has to stay here and hold our table. Since it's the last vacant one in the room."

That made sense, Grace decided.

"And then there's always the fact that we Southern boys like nothin' better than an excuse to pamper a gorgeous woman." He gave her another of those dashing buccaneer's smiles, then headed off toward the table, leaving her feeling a lot like Scarlett at the barbecue being waited on by the Tarleton twins.

Not that Lucas reminded her at all of those two hapless young men. He was definitely more Rhett Butler, she considered, watching as he crossed the room, seemingly oblivious to the admiring looks. Despite his south of the Mason-Dixon line drawl, she had no trouble imagining him in the role of that world-famous Yankee blockade runner.

"Who in the name of cover hunks everywhere is that?" a voice beside Grace suddenly asked.

Shaking off the fantasy of kissing Lucas while Atlanta went up in flames behind them, Grace looked up and managed a faint smile for her best friend.

"His name's Lucas Kincaid. And he's not a cover model."

"Lord, he should be. I know I write contemporaries,

but I've been toying with the idea of a time-travel featuring a pirate hero." Jamie Winston's eyes turned thoughtful. "I don't suppose—"

"No." Grace shook her head. "I don't think he's in the market for a career change."

"So, what does he do?" Jamie slipped into a chair beside Grace without taking her eyes from the object of her speculation. "And wherever did you find him?"

"In the classifieds."

"Lucky girl. All I've ever found in those ads is a used Plymouth and a kitten that needed to be wormed after we got her home. I guess I should have been looking under Hunks."

"Actually, I found him in the personals."

"While I'm pleased as punch that you're getting out again these days, I cannot believe a man who looks like that has to advertise for companionship."

"It's not that way. He was listed as a hero. And I needed one."

"Don't we all," Jamie drawled.

Grace laughed, relaxing for the first time in ages. "Well, there is that," she agreed. "But this was serious. Lucas is a bodyguard."

"Oh, no." Jamie Winston's smile faded from her face and from her eyes. "Don't tell me you've gotten another letter?"

"It was waiting for me here at the hotel when I arrived this morning."

Grace would never have considered withholding the truth from her best friend. She and Jamie had first met in Boston six years ago, at one of the few conferences Grace had attended. She had been a fledgling writer and Jamie already had half a dozen books under her jeweled belt.

A middle-of-the-night fire alarm at the hotel had forced them to climb down twenty-eight flights of stairs in their nightgowns. Grace hadn't even thought to grab her robe. Jamie, on the other hand, possessing a natural-born flair for the dramatic, had been swathed in ranch mink, which she'd willingly shared while they'd huddled together on the sidewalk on a cold New England night until the firemen had declared a false alarm.

That was how Grace discovered that Robert hadn't been in their room. Later, he'd assured her he'd been meeting with Buffy to discuss a possible anthology. Since she hadn't wanted to face the truth in those days, Grace hadn't pressed for details.

"I still don't think it's anything serious," she assured her friend. "But I was skimming through *USA Today* on the plane and saw this ad that asked, Need a Hero? Call 1-800-555-Hero. So I did."

"And you got him." Jamie's gaze wandered back across the room. "I never realized fairy godmothers had 1-800 numbers. Talk about modernizing."

Despite her reason for hiring Lucas in the first place, Grace laughed again. "I'm so glad you're here," she said with a warm rush of feeling.

"Where else would I be when my best pal wins a ROMI?" Jamie scowled. "It's only too bad that the Rat has to get one, too."

"The winners haven't been announced yet," Grace reminded her. "Besides, if it weren't for the Rat, I might never have gotten published in the first place."

Grace tried on occasion to remind herself that there'd been a time when Robert had been important to her. When she'd lived for his opinion, his approval. She certainly hadn't married him for the sex. Which had never been anything to shout about and was virtually nonexistent in the end.

"Hell, of course you would have. You're wonderfully talented, sweetie."

"Thank you. That means a lot from someone whose work I've always admired. But without his encouragement, I might have given up."

"Don't be ridiculous, you could no sooner quit writing than I could quit having babies." Jamie, who was pregnant with her fifth, patted her bulging stomach and smiled with feminine satisfaction. "Please tell me the hunk is single."

"I have no idea. It didn't come up."

"It's hard to believe women have let that one get away," Jamie mused. "Oh, Lord. This is San Francisco. You don't suppose he's gay, do you?"

"I have no idea. And I don't care." *Liar*, Grace thought as her own gaze wandered over to where Lucas was now surrounded by a bevy of admiring romance writers.

"Well, even if he is, there's no reason for anyone to ever know." Jamie's grin reminded Grace of a pregnant cat who'd just spotted a particularly succulent saucer of cream. "This situation is rife with possibilities for a delicious revenge."

"Revenge?"

"If Robert even remotely suspects there's anything personal going on between you two, he'll go nuts."

"If it doesn't have anything to do with my money, I doubt he'd even care."

"You're overlooking the wonderfully fragile male ego. Robert might have dumped you, but that doesn't mean that he isn't by nature competitive when it comes to women.

"It goes back to caveman days. Just because he was foolish enough to think he didn't want you doesn't mean he'll be able to stand the idea of some drop-dead-hunk Neanderthal whacking you over the head with a club and dragging you home to his cave."

"Lucas isn't exactly a Neanderthal."

"Don't be so picky. As a writer you should recognize a metaphor when you hear one. But believe me, Grace, when the Rat sees the two of you together, he'll undoubtedly go drown himself in the bay."

"One can only hope. Especially since Lucas changed my cover story from us being old friends to being old lovers."

"Oh, I just love this! It's right from the plot of my last book, where the bodyguard and the princess fall madly in love and live happily ever after."

"That's fiction," Grace noted dryly. "Just like Lucas's story."

"True. But don't forget that old saying about life imitating art," Jamie countered.

When she felt the hated telltale color rising in her cheeks again, Grace decided the time had come to change the subject. "By the way, did you hear that Robert's telling people he's going to be writing the new Scarlett book?"

"Not only did I hear, but Bubbles, his blushing bride, actually called me last week and asked me to write it for him."

"Her name's Buffy." As Jamie well knew.

"Buffy, Bubbles, Bimbo, it's all the same to me." Jamie dismissed the correction. "Anyway, she mentioned a very generous royalty split, but since the Rat is about as capable of crafting a story as an orangutan with a fistful of crayons, it was obvious I'd be left to do all the work while he went on *Good Morning America* and took all the glory. Something he's very good at. As you know all too well."

"Are you considering it?" Grace couldn't see where it would be a good career move. Then again, she didn't have any right to tell Jamie what—and with whom—she could write. Especially since her husband, Peter Winston, had recently given up a lucrative Chicago law practice to set up a storefront office in the inner city. And there was always the matter of another baby on the way.

"Are you kidding? Even if you weren't my best friend, and even if the Rat could write, which we both know he can't, there's no way I'd be willing to put up with his roving hands."

"Roving..." Grace stared at her long-time friend. "Surely you're not saying..."

"Aw, hell." Jamie shook her head. "I swore to myself that I was never going to say anything. But yeah, he hit on me a few times."

"When?"

"In Boston. And again in Chicago. And in Hawaii. And New York. Oh, and there were those brief little skirmishes we had in elevators in Dallas and Seattle."

"That's more than a few." It was every national RNN conference Robert had attended. Since Grace had felt uncomfortable in the spotlight, after the first year, she'd stayed home, content to let her husband, who enjoyed the publicity end of the business, take center stage. Which had left her free to write. And him to fool around. "Is that all?"

"Absolutely."

It was a lie and both women knew it.

Silence settled over them. "I should have told you," Jamie said glumly.

"Yeah. You should have."

"It was just that I valued our friendship so much I was afraid to risk his bad behavior coming between us."

She placed her hand on Grace's icy one.

"Besides, I didn't have any proof that he was cheating. And you know what an outrageous flirt he is. So I just kept trying to convince myself that he wasn't really serious about all those passes."

"Well, that certainly makes two of us." Grace sighed

and realized that she'd willingly overlooked the signs herself during the early days of her marriage. By the end, she'd suspected, but hadn't really cared.

"You know—" Jamie returned her gaze to Lucas, who seemed to be having a fascinating discussion about tempura shrimp with a flock of avid female admirers "—perhaps you could have the hunk beat him up."

Even as Grace told herself that she'd moved on with her life, she couldn't deny that the idea of Lucas pounding the stuffing out of Robert the Rat proved more than a little appealing.

When Lucas returned to the table with two gilt-rimmed plates, Grace made the introductions and was relieved when Jamie, who could be frighteningly outspoken, didn't utter a single word about the possibility of him modeling for her upcoming book cover. In fact, she seemed almost eager to leave them alone.

"It's a pleasure to meet you, Lucas."

"It's a pleasure to meet you," Lucas said, shaking the slender, outstretched hand. "As Gracie's best friend, you're probably just the lady to fill me in on any of the men in her life I might have to run off."

Jamie's eyes narrowed, then began to dance. "Gracie—" she drawled the nickname, seeming to enjoy it immensely "—has sworn off men."

Lucas nodded, pleased. "That's good to hear."

Not that he was concerned about any competition. Since he'd been seven years old and opened that lemonade stand in Raintree to buy his first bike, he'd always attained everything he wanted. As he'd watched Grace from across the room, he'd decided he wanted America's most beloved romance author. And he fully intended to have her.

"Lucas," Grace murmured, so as not to be overheard by the other writers at nearby tables, "I've already told Jamie the truth. You don't have to lie to her about our relationship."

"Who said I was lying?"

While Grace stared up at him, Jamie Winston's amused gaze went from Lucas to Grace, then back to Lucas again. Then finally settled on Grace. "Well, honey, for someone who's always avoided conferences, you've definitely found a way to make a huge splash at this one.

"And as much as I'm a sucker for real-life romance, I'm afraid I have an interview with Milan television in…" She glanced down at her watch. "Ten minutes ago." Her smile was quick and bright. "Fortunately for me, the Italians, bless their hearts, are never on time."

She stood up with amazing grace for a woman who made a habit of gaining fifty pounds with every pregnancy, then losing it in the first six postpartum weeks, something Grace could have hated her for if they hadn't been such close friends.

"I'm sure we'll run into each other before the conference is over, Lucas." Jamie bent down and brushed her lips against Grace's cheek. "I'm thrilled for you," she murmured. "I have a feeling this is going to be your most successful conference ever. And I'm not talking about the fact that you're a shoo-in for the ROMI."

"Lucas is just kidding," Grace insisted, shooting a frustrated look at the bodyguard, who, dammit, was grinning devilishly back at her. "Tell her, Lucas."

"Don't bother," Jamie said blithely. "Because I'd never believe it." She shifted her gaze from Grace's distressed face to Lucas again. "Grace is my best friend in the world. Break her heart and I'll hire a mobster to break your legs."

"You know, I almost think I believe you."

"You should. Because I mean every word." Warning given, she waggled her fingers. "Television Milan awaits. Have fun, you two."

Lucas watched as she paused to chat briefly with Alice Vail on her way out of the lounge. "Nice lady."

"The best," Grace said absently. His nonchalant manner almost had her believing she'd imagined his outrageous remark about running off any men in her life.

"You're lucky to have such a good friend."

"I know."

She tried to read his expression, which had turned frustratingly inscrutable. Surely she couldn't have invented the male interest that had darkened his eyes, thickened his drawl. Then again, she'd been under a great deal of stress lately. Perhaps she really was having a nervous breakdown.

"What did you mean by that?"

"By what?" Appearing oblivious to her turmoiled thoughts, Lucas took a bite of barbecued-duck pizza.

"What you said to Jamie. That threat about running off any men in my life."

"Oh, that." He shrugged. "Of course I meant it. But it wasn't a threat, Gracie. Merely a statement of intent."

"You're kidding." Amazed yet again at his matter-of-fact attitude, she let out a huff of breath. "I know you are."

"Well, that makes one of us." He tucked the errant strand of hair behind her ear again, pretending not to notice the way she stiffened at his touch. "Believe me, sugar, I may not have been a Boy Scout all my life, but I'd never lie to a woman about my intentions."

"I have no reason to believe you. Since I don't know you," she added.

"True enough. But don't worry, we can take care of that. I promise, darlin', that by the end of the conference, we'll be old friends. Old very close friends."

His easy drawl slipped beneath her skin in a way that set her nerves to humming again. For some reason she'd figure out later, when this strange fog cleared from her mind, Grace had to fight the urge to smile.

"Well, no one can fault you for your confidence."

"It's a Kincaid trait. Along with our natural-born charm."

"How strange," she said, beginning to enjoy herself, "I haven't noticed that."

"You probably haven't been paying close enough attention," he said helpfully. "Give me time, Gracie. I'll grow on you."

"Like algae."

He laughed, appearing absolutely unwounded. "So, your friend Jamie's a writer, too?"

"Yes." Grateful for the shift in subject, she bit into the fluffy fried dough of a shrimp tempura and could have wept, it was so good. "I met her at a conference, actually, when I first began writing."

"I guess that makes you competitors?"

"Competitors?"

"Yeah. Obviously, you're both in the business to sell books. What happens if one of you tops the charts?"

"We buy enough champagne to float a battleship and celebrate."

"So let's say that you had a book that made number one on the bestseller lists the same week she didn't make the top ten. Would that prove a problem?"

Grace was puzzled at the way the easy, flirtatious conversation had suddenly turned oddly serious. "Not at all. Our friendship has never been based on numbers, and besides, we don't even write the same sort of books."

"They're both romance."

"True. But hers are short contemporary stories for Harlequin's Temptation line and mine are historicals. But it wouldn't matter. Because we still only want the best for each other."

"And she feels the same way?"

"Of course."

He took another bite of pizza without taking his gaze from hers. He looked inclined to ask another question when a cocktail waitress appeared beside the table, pad in hand, pen poised.

"What would you like to drink?" Lucas asked.

"I'll have a glass of chardonnay." Grateful for the interruption, Grace ignored Lucas and gave her order directly to the waitress.

"And I'll have a Coke," he said. "Thanks."

Grace reluctantly gave him points for not watching the young woman's long slender legs, clad in black stockings, as she walked away.

"And here I would have guessed you to be a Southern Comfort man."

"You would have guessed right, once upon a time. These days I don't drink period." He picked up a mushroom stuffed with Dungeness crab and popped it into his mouth. "You mentioned buying enough champagne to float a battleship? Well, I used to drink enough to float an entire flotilla."

"But you stopped?"

"Yeah. One day about eighteen months ago, I poured the booze down the drain and have been on the wagon ever since."

"Wasn't that difficult? Quitting cold turkey?" Having researched alcoholism for a book she'd written, Grace suspected there was a great deal Lucas wasn't telling her.

"It came down to life-style. I got tired of waking up every morning with the mother of all hangovers. So I decided the best way to avoid the hangover was to avoid the alcohol in the first place."

"Why did you drink?"

"Because I was a drunk." Lucas decided this was neither the time nor the place to discuss the nightmares that had haunted him after his final mission.

The waitress returned with their drinks. The smile the long-legged brunette bestowed on Lucas was warm, inviting and caused an unfamiliar jolt of jealousy Grace had never experienced when she'd been married to Robert. Even when he'd run off with Buffy, Grace had honestly been more devastated by the loss of her editor than her husband.

"So." Lucas lifted his glass. "To a successful conference."

Since she now had a very good idea what he'd consider successful, Grace decided the time had come to inform him yet again that she had no intention of warming his bed the next few nights.

"Speaking of that—"

"There you are!" The all-too-familiar male voice cut into her intended speech. "How the hell did you do it? That's what I want to know."

Grace looked up at her former husband, took in his face, which was as red as a boiled crab, and wondered what she'd ever seen in this man. Oh, she supposed he was handsome enough, in what she now knew to be a pseudointellectual sort of way. He was tall and lean, but without Lucas's rangy strength. His eyes, reddened by the contact lenses he'd taken to wearing for television appearances, were currently shooting furious sparks, and his lips were pulled into that thin, disapproving line she remembered all too well.

"Do what?" She did not bother with pleasantries, since there was absolutely nothing about this man she found pleasant.

"Steal my suite out from under me."

"What?" She shot a quick look at Lucas, who merely

shrugged and turned his attention to the popcorn shrimp. Surely, he wouldn't...he couldn't... Could he?

"Actually, Robert, if you insist on bringing the subject up, it just happens to be you who stole *my* suite."

"It was reserved in the Roberta Grace name," he reminded her as he plucked a square of Swiss cheese from her plate. It was something he'd always done. Something that had also always annoyed her. "Which makes it as much mine as it is yours."

"Aren't you a little old to be claiming Finders Keepers, Losers Weepers?" Lucas asked mildly.

"Who the hell are you?"

"Lucas Kincaid." He did not extend his hand. Grace watched, intrigued, as a spooky, silent warning seemed to rise in his dark eyes. "The new guy in Gracie's life. Who, by the way, suggests that if you want to live, you refrain from speaking that way to my woman."

"Your woman? Gracie?" When his jaw actually dropped, Grace wondered why she'd never noticed how weak it was.

Seeming to forget his initial complaint, Robert swung his attention back to Grace. "I cannot believe that a woman with your intelligence would stoop to sleeping with some..." he paused, fuming as he searched for the right word "...hunk!" Obviously piqued, he snatched a mushroom.

It did not escape Grace's notice that he'd called her intelligent. Something he hadn't done since their early days together. Heaven help her for being a petty person, but she actually found herself thoroughly enjoying the moment.

"I fail to see how what I do is any of your business," she countered, conveniently overlooking the fact that she had no intention of sleeping with Lucas. "Now, I believe you were complaining about the accommodations?"

As if remembering Lucas's warning, Robert drew in a deep breath and forced his voice to a less accusing tone. "I just went up to the suite to make a few phone calls and discovered Buffy's and my things being moved out. And yours moved in! When I asked what they thought they were doing, I was informed that the order had come directly from the manager. Naturally, I sought him out immediately."

"Naturally," she murmured, still uncertain what exactly had happened, but continuing to suspect that somehow Lucas had had a hand in it.

"He informed me that there'd been a mixup and the room was originally reserved for you."

"He was right."

"That's open to interpretation." Robert waved her statement away with an irritated gesture that caused her to notice the diamond wedding band he was wearing. The wedding band that he and Buffy had obviously purchased with his unearned share of her royalties. "And you want to know the worst part?"

"Not particularly." Her dry tone caused Lucas to pat her knee approvingly beneath the table. The touch, while meant as encouragement, seemed intensely intimate.

"Every damn room in the hotel is booked. And since it's the holiday weekend, the best the guy could do was get me a room at the Marriott on the Wharf."

Lucas's hand was stroking her thigh now, in a way that sent little sparks through her bloodstream. "That's a nice hotel." Grace was amazed that her words didn't come out in a croak.

"It's not the Whitfield Palace," he complained.

"True," Grace murmured, wondering at what temperature the human body melted. She was concerned that if Lucas kept touching her like this, she was about to find out.

"You know, Radcliffe, if you're going to settle into the Marriott and make it back here for the pageant on time, you'd better get moving," Lucas suggested. He skimmed his fingers back down Grace's thigh and cupped her knee again. "Traffic's always tough this time of day. And it's hard to get a cab."

Again, his reasonable tone belied what actually appeared to be a potential for violence in his steady eyes. As Grace watched her former husband wisely opt not to challenge that look, she couldn't help wondering how Lucas was capable of threatening Robert at the same time his wickedly clever hand was caressing her beneath the table.

Unaware of the intimate little drama taking place between Lucas and his former wife, Robert shot Grace a lethal glare that jolted her nerves and started them jittering, then turned on his heel and marched away from the table.

4

"ARE YOU ALL RIGHT?" Lucas asked quietly. He'd been aware of her tension, had felt her skin turn to ice.

"Yes." Her voice was calm. As she picked up her wineglass to take a calming sip, her hands were not.

"Would you like me to go after him and rip out his cheating heart?"

His matter-of-fact tone stunned her. "Of course not."

He shrugged. "Your choice."

But he would have. Willingly. And enjoyed bringing it back to her on a silver platter, like some knight returning home from the Crusades. The funny thing was, Lucas had never considered himself a shining-armor kind of guy.

Which must mean, he decided with grim humor, that being around all these fancifully dressed women was playing havoc with his imagination. And being with Grace, breathing in her light springtime scent, was creating havoc not only with his mind, but his body as well.

"You're kidding." She stared at him, her glass halfway between her rosy lips and the table. "Lucas, please tell me you're not serious."

"Okay. I'm not serious," he lied.

She gave him another longer look. Then managed a faint smile. "You're just trying to make me feel better."

"Absolutely." That was definitely the truth. He was also, he reminded himself, determined to keep her alive.

Lucas had learned to trust his instincts, and his first impression had been that Radcliffe, while full of bluster, was incapable of having the guts to actually kill anyone. But after witnessing that hot, lethal glare, as if the guy had been fantasizing putting his pale, patrician fingers around Grace's neck, Lucas put the ex-husband back at the top of his prime suspect list.

"What did you ever see in that guy, anyway?"

"I've asked myself the same question." She managed a half laugh and took another sip of wine. When he didn't say anything, just kept looking at her with that patient, unwavering gaze, she knew he was waiting for more.

She sighed and decided to get it over with, since she suspected he wasn't going to drop the subject. And again, rather than have him pick up false rumors, she'd rather he hear the truth from her. "I met Robert when I was a junior at Princeton."

"Nice school." And pricey, he thought, wondering if she was some rich man's little princess, and if so, why her father hadn't stepped in to rescue her.

"I was a scholarship student," she said, unknowingly answering his question. "My father was a fisherman on Chesapeake Bay."

"Was?"

"He died in a squall when I was thirteen."

A tender age, he thought. A young girl on the threshold of womanhood. "I'm sorry."

"So was I." Her smile was soft and a little sad. "My mother moved us to Kansas the day after the funeral. She was—and still is—a legal secretary in Wichita. I've suggested she retire and enjoy her life, since I could certainly support her, but she loves her work."

"She must be proud of you."

"Yes." This time the smile lit her remarkable eyes, turning them that warm turquoise hue again. "She is."

He could kiss her, Lucas considered, as desire curled in his gut. Right now, he could just lower his head and touch

his mouth to hers. It would be so easy. And so complicated, because he suspected that one kiss wasn't going to
be enough.

"You were telling me about your ex." When he discovered he definitely didn't like the idea of any other man
touching Grace, kissing those full lips, making love to her,
Lucas reminded himself that jealousy clouded the mind.
Which was definitely something he couldn't afford.

"Are you asking because you consider him a suspect?"

"That's one reason. Another is that I'm interested in
why a gorgeous, intelligent woman who obviously has so
much going for her could have ever gotten tied up with
such a bastard."

"He didn't seem a bastard when I fell in love with
him." Or thought she had. "I'd never met anyone like
Robert. Most of the boys I knew in Kansas were in the cat-
tle business. And in Maryland they either grew up to be
fishermen, like their fathers, or joined the merchant ma-
rine."

She smiled briefly at that. "There must be something in
the air in that part of the country that draws people to the
sea. I wanted to be a sailor when I was nine."

"I was in the navy," he admitted, surprising himself by
revealing the fact. As a rule, he didn't talk about those
days. "And believe me, sugar, having you on board a ship
definitely would have improved the view during those
months at sea."

She could have been offended. If any other man had
made such a chauvinistic statement, she undoubtedly
would have been. But since it was Lucas, she chose instead to be pleased by the compliment. She also decided
that, since he was already cocky enough, there was no
point in encouraging him by responding to his flattering
words.

"Anyway, Princeton seemed like a different planet

from either world I'd grown up in. The worlds I was comfortable with. Although I had no trouble keeping up with the classwork and made good grades, I felt so out of place I spent the first two years hiding away in the library when I wasn't in class."

Lucas had never considered the benefits of being a librarian. Until now.

"Then I met Robert."

Her right hand was still in Lucas's. Since it felt strangely right there, Grace ran the fingers of her left around the rim of her wineglass as she thought back to those long-ago days. "He was my English lit professor."

"I can see this one coming a mile away."

"It is rather a cliché, isn't it?" she asked dryly, and with a hint of self-disdain. "He was the most sophisticated man I'd ever met. He was witty, urbane, smoked a pipe—"

"Wore natty tweed sport coats with leather elbow patches," Lucas guessed.

"Yes." Grace smiled, not at the memory, but at her girlish foolishness at mistaking yet another cliché for sophistication.

"I suppose he was also working on the great American novel."

"Actually, he'd already written a historical saga about the Industrial Revolution. It had been making the rounds of publishers for several years without success."

Grace recalled the first time she'd read the poorly written manuscript, at Robert's redbrick home just off campus. Remembered sympathizing with him over glasses of white wine about publishing philistines who were interested more in commercial pap than true literary genius. That had also been the night she'd lost her virginity on his chocolate brown leather sofa.

"So the New York publishing world didn't exactly find that a scintillating topic?"

"Let's just say that they weren't enthusiastic about Robert's version. As it happens, I was working on a novel based on the same time period."

"Nice coincidence."

"I certainly thought so at the time." She definitely wasn't about to reveal she'd romantically mistaken it as a sign of fate that she'd found her literary soul mate. "Of course I was thrilled when he offered to share his research."

"Generous guy. Was that before or after he'd read your manuscript?"

How quickly he'd caught on, Grace thought, wondering yet again how she could have been so naive. So foolish.

"After." Although she hated to admit it, even to herself, until she'd submitted her first chapters for a writing exercise, Robert had scarcely noticed she was alive, preferring to bestow his attention on the petite, flirtatious blondes in the first row. She'd been neither petite nor flirtatious. In fact, she'd been frankly overweight and painfully shy.

Ransomed Hearts was a romantic romp depicting the adventures of a down-on-his-luck highwayman and his kidnap victim, whose wealthy family didn't want her back.

"Since Robert was so eager to help, and it was exciting having someone to talk with about my story, I incorporated into my book a few of the facts he'd compiled." About two paragraphs, in a 150,000-word book.

"It was accepted for publication by Penbrook Press the week I graduated. Since Robert thought I should save my real name for later, serious work, and he'd been so supportive, I agreed that his idea of using Roberta Grace as a pseudonym was a sensible solution."

"But you said earlier that he didn't actually do any writing."

"No. Not really." Sometimes Grace wondered how any woman could have been so gullible. Let alone one who'd graduated from an Ivy League university summa cum laude. "Neither of us expected the book to be such a success. Suddenly, I felt as if I were on a runaway train racing downhill...."

"There were interviews, media tours, reader parties." She saw no need to mention throwing up before nearly every one. "As I said, I'm not very extroverted." That was undoubtedly the understatement of the millennium. "And as Robert pointed out, I didn't exactly fit the image of a romance writer."

It still hurt, Grace realized. Embarrassed at sharing that humiliating part of her life with a man she'd just met, especially one who looked as if he could have stepped out of the pages of one of her books, she dragged her gaze back out the window and wished she could suddenly beam herself aboard one of those sleek white boats cruising across the bay.

She remembered her father taking her sailing on the Chesapeake when she'd been a girl. Even now, her memories of those halcyon days remained so strong and appealing she didn't need a psychologist to point out that she'd based all her heroes on the bold, larger-than-life man she'd adored.

"I'll have to agree with the Rat on that point." Lucas skimmed a look over her. "You're definitely no dowager swathed in pink chiffon ruffles and dripping with diamonds."

She laughed, feeling the little cloud of depression that had been threatening to settle over her lift. "That's one unfortunate stereotype. But actually, I was thinking more along the lines of the character Morgan Fairchild plays on "Friends." A size-two blond glamour queen poured into sequined spandex?" she added when he appeared not to recognize the role.

"Never watched the show. But I've always found sequined spandex to be overkill. And though I'm admittedly clueless about women's sizes, as far as I'm concerned, you look pretty perfect."

It was ridiculous, Grace thought, to receive such pleasure from a glib compliment the man undoubtedly handed out often and indiscriminately. Ridiculous and foolish, and dangerous. "That's very flattering."

"It's the truth," he said simply. Then he lifted her fingers to his lips. "Radcliffe's a fool, Gracie. He didn't deserve you then, and he damn well doesn't deserve you now."

The touch of his lips on her skin was warming her blood, but Grace kept her eyes on his. "I know."

The awareness was there, humming between them, impossible to resist. "It'd probably cause a scene if I kissed you right here in front of everyone."

"Absolutely," she insisted. She drew in a breath. Released it. But did not back away.

He cupped her cheek and felt the heat rise, like a candle flame burning beneath white satin. "And you're not a woman who likes to make scenes."

"No." Her foolish heart had begun to flutter like a wild bird in her chest. "I'm not."

His smile was slow. Sensual. Devastating. "Too bad. Because I have a feeling that's going to be inevitable, before this conference ends."

He lowered his head, watching the way her huge wary eyes turned to the jeweled hue of emeralds. "Fascinating," he murmured.

"What?" The whisper escaped on a soft, stuttering breath.

"Your eyes." He skimmed his thumb in the shadowed hollow between her lower lashes and cheek. "I've been trying to decide what color they are."

"Hazel." She swallowed. Licked her lips and realized her error when hunger flashed in his watchful, midnight eyes. "They're hazel."

"Technically, perhaps." The enticing touch trailed down her cheek, brushed against lips that had already gone dry again. "But they change. Like when we were downstairs in the oyster bar, they seemed blue. But in the elevator, on the way up here, I decided they were turquoise."

His fingers were callused, like the finest grade of sandpaper. Although she'd never considered herself a very physical woman, they were making her ache to feel them all over her body.

"And now they're as green as emeralds." His mouth hovered a whisper away from hers. "As deep as the sea."

"We can't...I can't... You c-c-can't." Grace had thought she'd outgrown her childhood stutter.

"Yes." Her lips parted beneath his thumb, silently inviting the kiss she was trying to insist she did not want. "I can." He watched her eyes darken. "You can." His tantalizing touch journeyed to the corner of her mouth. "And we will."

"Lucas...please."

"Please yes? Or please no?"

He suspected she meant the latter. But she was wrong. This had been inevitable from the minute he'd walked into Neptune's Table. No, Lucas decided, before that. When he'd stayed at the office that extra five minutes, strangely unwilling to leave, which had him there to take

Samantha's call. He'd never been a man who believed in destiny. Never trusted in fate. Until now.

When she didn't immediately answer, he made the decision for her, for both of them. "Later," he decided. "It's probably best without the audience." Unwilling to give up contact, he skimmed his thumb over her lips one last time. Then sighed. "Besides, you still have to change before this evening's festivities. And although you look gorgeous just the way you are, you'll undoubtedly want time to primp."

Once again his compliment sent a rush of unbidden pleasure through her. Lord, Grace thought, she was hopeless. A single look, or touch, or word from this man was all it took to turn her into Silly Putty. She was going to have to work on that. Really she was. Beginning now.

"You're right." She reminded herself that she was a strong, independent woman. A woman who had gained control over her life. Because her pulse was still jittery, she forced herself to look straight into his dark, devilish eyes. "This conference is important to me, Mr. Kincaid. I have a great deal riding on it, along with responsibilities I can't put aside to play games with you."

"For the record, sugar, I don't play games."

The flirtatious tone was gone from his voice. It was rough, and edged with a frustration that had darkened his eyes to almost black. Once again her system jolted; once again she managed to steady it. Just barely.

"My point was," she said, her voice cool, her eyes frost, "I do not have time for a dalliance, an affair, or a quick roll in the hay—"

"Believe me, Gracie, when I do take you to bed, there'll be nothing quick about it."

Oh, she did. Absolutely. And that, of course, was part of the problem. "As I was saying," she said, forging on, "you're a distraction I can't afford. If you keep talking to me like this, I'm going to have to call S. J. Slade and request another bodyguard."

Lucas was not at all wild about being called a distraction. But he also wasn't one to blow a job. Even one he hadn't wanted in the first place.

"Better watch what buttons you push, Gracie," he advised mildly. "Unless you want to discover exactly how much of a distraction I can be." He pushed back from the table, rose, folded his arms and looked down at her. "Ready to go?"

Heaven help her, her rebellious body, which seemed to have taken on a mind of its own, was actually responding to that veiled threat. What on earth was wrong with her? Hadn't she learned anything after her debacle of a marriage? The last time she'd been so charmed by a man had turned out disastrously.

But she was no longer an insecure, foolhardy young girl. She was a grown woman, successful beyond her wildest childhood dreams. Surely she was capable of handling Lucas Kincaid. It was, after all, only three days. Three days during which she was going to be incredibly busy. So busy she'd hardly even notice Lucas was with her.

As she pushed herself to her feet, stifling the oath that was dancing on the tip of her tongue, it occurred to Grace that ignoring Lucas would undoubtedly be a great deal easier said than done.

Paying scant heed to her earlier admonition, Lucas put a blatantly proprietary hand on her waist as he ushered her past the tables of romance writers, all of whom eyed the couple with open speculation.

Neither spoke as they waited for the elevator. But the tension hovered between them like a live wire. Grace breathed a sigh of relief when, after what seemed an eternity, it finally reached their floor and opened with a hiss of the doors. They entered, and as the doors closed again, Lucas pushed the button.

"You can't tell me you haven't been wondering," he said as he watched the numbers flash above the door.

"Wondering about what?"

"What it would be like. Me kissing you." His gaze drifted to her face, skimmed down to her lips. "You kissing me back."

"Lucas—" she warned, holding up a hand like a traffic cop "—don't you dare...."

"Too late." He gathered her close, covered her mouth with his and took what he wanted.

Lucas had kissed other women before. More than he cared to count. But none of them had ever instantly fogged his brain, as was happening now. He'd suspected she'd be sweet. And she was. Sweet and succulent and delicious. But he hadn't been prepared for the punch that followed the initial taste.

Uncharacteristically unsure of his footing, like a man backing away from the jagged edge of a steep precipice, he drew away, just far enough to see her eyes, which blinked open at the sudden separation. They were dark and dazed and revealed both shock and a wariness he could identify with.

He wanted her. Wildly. Worse yet, he needed her. Desperately. Both were something he was going to have to think about later, when his thoughts had cleared and his body stopped feeling as if cluster bombs were exploding inside it.

"Well." Unwilling to give up complete contact, he trailed a fingertip along the edge of her top lip and was rewarded by her slight tremor. "That was certainly a surprise."

"Not a pleasant one." It wasn't exactly a lie, Grace assured herself. Pleasant didn't begin to describe his kiss.

Mind blinding, perhaps. Earth-shattering. But pleasant? No way.

"Should I apologize?" With her blood still pounding in her ears, his steady voice—how dare he be calm, when she was so shaken!—sounded as if it were coming from the bottom of the sea.

Grace knew she could have stopped the kiss. Should have stopped it. But as his head had lowered slowly, inexorably toward hers, she'd told herself it was only a test. Of course she was curious. What female wouldn't be? Lucas Kincaid was the kind of man women dreamed about, the kind romance writers wrote stories about. The problem was, she'd come to the conclusion that such dashing heroes that populated the pages of her books didn't exist in real life.

"No." Her voice was ragged. Shaky. Grace hated it. She drew in a breath meant to calm, then tried again. "But there's one thing we need to get straight."

"All right."

"I realize that men think that because a woman writes romance novels, she's always in the mood for research, but—"

"Is that what you think that kiss was about?" Anger steamrolled over any lingering desire. Since it kept him from groveling, Lucas welcomed it.

The cold fury in his eyes affected her far more strongly than Robert's earlier hot glare. Lucas's words fell between them like chips of ice, belying the earlier warmth of his mouth.

"Wasn't it?"

Reminding himself that his assignment was to keep her alive, which he could hardly do if he ran her off the first night of the conference, Lucas managed, just barely, to control another wave of temper. "Hell, no."

"I'm sorry if I jumped to the wrong conclusion. It's just that some men—"

"Now there you go," he drawled. "Shooting those little barbs at my ego again by lumping me in with a bunch of cretins who might hit on a lady just because of the mistaken idea she has sex on her mind."

There was no way Grace was going to admit that she knew very few women who could be in such close proximity to Lucas Kincaid and not harbor sexual thoughts.

"Then why did you kiss me?"

"Because you're gorgeous, sexy, spunky as hell beneath that Princess Grace composure, and because you smell pretty darn good, too. But most of all, I did it to please myself. And hopefully, to please you."

Oh, it had certainly done that. But it had also shaken her to her toes. "Well, it can't happen again."

"Why not?"

"Because we've both come here with a job to do. A job that doesn't involve fooling around."

"Haven't you ever heard of mixing work and play?"

"Yes. It's just that I've never believed in it."

He shook his head. "That is, without a doubt, the most pitiful thing I've ever heard."

The deep drawl took the sting out of the accusation, and the renewed teasing glint in his eyes drew a faint smile of her own.

"I can't picture you being in the navy...following orders," she elaborated, when he lifted a questioning dark brow.

"Sometimes my commanding officers couldn't see it, either. When I wasn't real good about following orders." He didn't add that in the world of covert operations, where the men sent into dangerous locales in the middle of the night often had to make up the plan on the spot, things were a lot looser. Which was the only reason he'd managed to last as long as he had. "That's one of the reasons I left."

"To become a bodyguard."

"Yeah." He didn't mention that he'd been planning to quit the bodyguard gig until he walked into the oyster bar and met her.

She angled her head, studying him. "From my conversation with Samantha Slade, I have the distinct impression that you may have jumped out of that proverbial frying pan into the fire. She sounded like a very formidable woman."

"She is that," Lucas agreed. "And speaking of fires, I have to warn you, Gracie, that I'm suddenly struck with another urge to kiss you."

"Resist it," she advised as she exited the elevator, ignoring the interested glances of writers she thankfully didn't personally know.

When Lucas started walking down the hallway with her, she stopped and looked up at him. "What do you think you're doing?"

"Walking you to your suite."

"That's not necessary."

"Of course it is." He put a hand on her waist again. "My daddy always taught me to treat a lady with manners. Which, in my book, means walking her home after stealing a kiss."

"If you have to steal that kiss, perhaps your manners need a little work in the first place," Grace suggested dryly.

"Now there's a thought," Lucas agreed. "But since I can't ever recall a time when the lady didn't honestly want to be kissed, I'm not quite certain it fits the circumstances."

From the way she'd responded, Grace knew she'd never get away with insisting that she hadn't wanted Lucas to kiss her. "I may have been curious," she admitted. "But that's all."

"So, has your curiosity been satisfied?"

When the devils began dancing in those midnight dark eyes again, Grace resumed walking. "Absolutely."

With his long stride, Lucas had no difficulty catching up with her. "And?"

"Are you asking for a scorecard?"

"Sure. And please be gentle. You know what delicate egos we males possess."

Personally, Grace had already decided that Lucas's ego was armor plated. "It was nice."

"Nice?" Damn. Cocker spaniels were nice. A hot dog at the ballpark was nice. TV weathermen were nice. "If that was the best you can say, then perhaps I ought to try again."

"That's not necessary," she said quickly. Too quickly, Lucas thought with satisfaction.

The prudent thing to do would have been to lie. And, with the exception of her foolish marriage to Robert, she'd always thought of herself as a prudent woman. Until now.

"Actually, I suppose, if I were to be perfectly honest, it was *very* nice."

"I can do a lot better than that."

"Why don't I just take your word for that?" She'd reached the double doors to the suite and slipped the key card Robert had thrown down on the table into the slot. The light blinked green, allowing her to open the door.

Ignoring her muffled complaint, Lucas blithely brushed by her and walked into the suite as if he owned it.

"I don't recall inviting you in," she said, watching in amazement as he crossed the room and opened the door to the bedroom.

"Just checking the place out. After all, I wouldn't want it said that any client didn't get her money's worth." He opened the mirrored closet door, then crouched down and checked under the bed, which, he was pleased to see, had one of those solid wooden frames. Satisfied, he opened the adjoining bathroom door.

"Cool tub," he called to her. "And big enough to swim laps in." He glanced back over his shoulder and waggled his eyebrows in a deliberately roguish way. "Or for any other indoor sports you might want to indulge in."

"That's it."

Grace took hold of his wide shoulders, turned him toward the door and marched him back through the bedroom to the living room, which offered a dazzling view. Dusk was settling over the city, and the lights from cars on the streets far below looked like fallen stars.

"Now that you've determined some crazed killer isn't hiding beneath my bed or in the tub, it's time for you to leave. I still have to unpack and get changed for the pageant."

"You're the one calling the shots," he said with an agreeability Grace didn't trust for a minute. He deftly ducked from beneath her touch and checked out the bathroom off the foyer. Just in case. "So, what time do you want me to pick you up?

"I'll be here," he promised after she'd named a time. "And meanwhile, if you need anything—like help washing that hard-to-reach spot in the middle of your back, or a hand zipping up your dress—just knock on the wall."

"The wall?" Suspicion stirred. No, she thought, the coincidence would be impossible. There were three thousand rooms in the hotel and the conference must have booked nearly two-thirds of those. "Where is your room, anyway?"

"Didn't I mention that?"

"No." Oh, he was good, Grace thought. Smooth and slick, with that good-old-boy grin and Southern charm that made it difficult to get a good ire going. She folded her arms. "You didn't."

"As it happens, I'm staying in the next room." He knocked lightly on the closed door that, if unlocked, would turn the single-bedroom suite into a two-bedroom one. "Right on the other side of this door, as a matter of fact. Handy, isn't it?"

"How did you do it?"

"Do what?"

Grace set her teeth when she wanted to grind them. "Get Robert kicked out of here, me moved in and you booked into the room next door."

"I told you, darlin', when you hire S. J. Slade, you get the best," he assured her. "Wait till you sample a few of my other talents."

Grace had a very good idea exactly what type of talents he was referring to. She was about to insist, yet again, that he stop trying to seduce her when the grandfather clock in the corner of the living room signaled with a peal of Westminster chimes the passing of precious time.

"I can't deny I'm grateful, for whatever you did to get Robert evicted," she said. "But since I'm the one paying a very hefty fee for your services, I'd appreciate you sharing any of your plans with me ahead of time."

"I've been up front with you from the beginning," he said as she pushed him the rest of the way out of the foyer. "About all my intentions, Gracie."

His voice had dropped into that low, sexy timbre again. "And stop talking to me like that!" She practically slammed the door behind him and turned the lock.

"Don't forget to latch the chain, darlin'," he called in to her.

Swearing beneath her breath, Grace did as instructed. But not because he'd told her so.

Frustrated, and, dammit, fascinated by the hard-headed, hard-bodied man, she leaned back against the locked door and closed her eyes.

Then heard Lucas chuckle as he walked away.

5

GRACE ONLY BOTHERED to unpack those few things that needed to be hung up, then took a quick in-and-out shower, not even waiting for the water to warm up. After redoing her makeup and hair, she hurriedly dressed for the costume pageant.

All the time she couldn't get Lucas's staggering kiss out of her mind. Although she'd been married, he could have been her first. The first man to ever look at her as if she was the only woman in the world, the first man to want her, the first to kiss her. That had been her sole thought as she'd watched his mouth approach hers. And then, as their lips had touched, she'd forgotten to think at all.

Composure and control had always been important to Grace. Well, not always, she amended, thinking back to the way, as a child, she'd loved nothing more than to be aboard her father's sloop, the two of them facing the wind, skimming along the deep blue water so fast it felt like flying.

But then he was gone, taken by the very sea he'd loved. And her mother had moved to Kansas, as far from either ocean as she could get. She'd also made it her maternal duty to point out to Grace at every opportunity that risk inevitably ended in a loss of control. And disaster.

When Grace heard Lucas knock on her door, she tried to remind herself that allowing herself to become involved with a rogue of a man who could warm her blood with a single look, and make her mind float with his kisses, would represent the greatest risk of her life.

She'd have to remember that, she vowed, as she spritzed on some scent from a crystal bottle.

She took her time, forcing him to wait out in the hall. He'd been incredibly high-handed from the moment she'd met him; it would do him good to have to cool his heels, to realize that she wasn't going to jump when he snapped his long, callused fingers, or melt into a puddle of need every time he looked at her with those dark, strangely unfathomable eyes.

Her eyes seemed brighter than usual, and a color that had nothing to do with the blush she'd applied with a light hand rode high on her cheekbones. She looked edgy, expectant, even high-strung, which was surprising, since she'd always considered herself a levelheaded, remarkably unemotional person compared to most other writers. If she'd been describing herself as a character tonight she might have compared herself to a Thoroughbred at the starting gate.

"More like a Clydesdale," she muttered, narrowing her eyes at the rounded curves that were a far cry from current fashion.

Deciding that there was no way she could lose twenty pounds in the next minute, and knowing that Lucas was not going to go downstairs without her, she sighed, reassured herself that her nervousness was due to her public appearance and had nothing to do with Lucas Kincaid, then finally went to answer the door before the object of all her distraction broke it down. Which, oddly, since she had no proof that he could be a violent man, she feared he just might.

"What took you so long?"

When she hadn't immediately responded to his knock, horrifying images had flashed through Lucas's mind:

mental photographs of Grace drowned in the bathtub, stabbed beside that antique canopied and draped bed, lying dead on the plush carpeting, blood pouring forth from a bullet wound in her breast.

Having never lost a client, he wasn't about to begin with her, which was why he'd been on the verge of breaking down her door and, if necessary, explaining his behavior later.

"I was getting dressed."

He'd changed as well, appearing both sophisticated and dangerous in his navy suit and starched white collarless shirt. Unsurprisingly, he'd forgone a tie. Because just looking at him towering over her, made her mouth almost water, Grace forced her voice to a cooler tone than usual.

Although she knew she was being ridiculously fanciful, she pictured him on the deck of a pirate ship, clad in a billowy white shirt unfastened to reveal a hard dark chest, his jet hair, freed from its leather thong, whipping wildly in the sea breeze. She could almost smell the salty tang of the air.

Deciding the fantasy stemmed from the fact that she was currently plotting a pirate story, Grace reminded herself that while she wrote romance novels, she'd never had any problem separating fantasy from reality. Until now.

Obviously, the horrid letters she'd been receiving really had pushed her to the verge of a nervous breakdown. And wouldn't that make dandy tabloid headlines?

As he took in the sight of her, dressed in a silk dress the color of autumn leaves that was draped to display her lush body to advantage, Lucas felt every atom in his body begin to warm.

"You look drop-dead gorgeous."

"Thank you." The intimacy in his eyes echoed the compliment, causing another perilous spike in her hormones.

Grace managed, just barely, to resist wiping her suddenly damp hands on her skirt.

"Don't thank me. Thank whatever Valkyrie contributed to your gene pool."

If she'd wanted to drive him crazy all night, she couldn't have chosen better ammunition. The neckline of the dress skimmed her collarbone in a way that enhanced the contrast between her porcelain pale skin and the bronze material. It was pinched in at the waistline, all the better to accentuate her hourglass figure, then ended abruptly midway down her thighs, revealing long wrap-around legs that had him almost biting his tongue.

Her heels were dangerously high and spindly, putting her almost at eye level with him. All the better to watch that unbidden awareness rise in those thickly lashed eyes that were rapidly turning green with desire.

Because he knew he'd be thinking of little else all night, and telling himself that he'd need a clear head to protect her, Lucas took two steps into the room and, without taking his gaze from hers, kicked the door closed behind him.

As he crushed his mouth against hers, Grace was instantly engulfed by titanic waves of passion that pounded against the composure she'd struggled for years to achieve. His kiss rocked her, sent her reeling, tumbling helpless beneath those perilous waves as if she'd been pulled beneath the tow of a riptide.

She heard a low, throaty moan that she didn't recognize as her own, was only dimly aware of his hands digging into the silk at her waist as he pulled her tighter against him, pressing her curves against his hard, rangy body.

The feel of her arched and straining against him, the taste of her, as sweet as honey, as potent as whiskey, the desperate little moans torn from her throat—all these things tangled together, coalescing into a hunger that left Lucas blind with need.

He wanted to drag her to the floor, to tear that silk dress from her body, to feel her naked and writhing beneath him. He wanted to bury himself deep inside her, to drive her senseless, to hear her cry out his name at the moment of climax. And then he wanted to take her again. And again, until they were both limp and drained and satiated.

And because he wanted all that with a desperation like nothing he'd ever known, Lucas managed to pull away from the brink of madness.

"We have to stop doing this." Her hands trembled as she touched her fingertips to her temples. "Believe it or not, I've never responded so recklessly to a man's kisses before in my life."

"If you're trying to bolster my ego, Gracie," he drawled, enjoying hearing her confirm what he'd already suspected, "you're definitely going about it in the right way."

A sound that was half laugh, half sob escaped her ravished lips. They stood there, inches apart, the energy between them as palpable as the lightning preceding a squall.

"I'll be right back." Needing a moment to garner her scattered composure, Grace returned to the bathroom to check her appearance. Unsurprisingly, Lucas was right on her heels.

As he came up behind her, Grace was tempted to remind him that she hadn't invited him into her bathroom, then realized that by responding to his kiss with such unbridled passion, she'd invited a great deal more.

"I look a mess," she moaned, touching up her lipstick.

"On the contrary. You look like a woman who's been

thoroughly kissed." He smiled encouragingly at her in the mirror.

"That's just the point." She resecured a few tendrils of hair that had sprung loose from her French braid, jabbing pins into her scalp. "The minute we walk into that room together they'll know exactly what we've been doing—"

"And be as jealous as hell."

"I really do have to stop feeding your ego," she muttered, snatching up a tube of blush. "Did it ever cross your mind that not every woman at this conference might want to sleep with you?"

"No. I haven't thought along those lines because I'm not interested in sleeping with every woman at this conference. The only one I want is you, Gracie." He plucked the blush from her hand and put it back onto the dressing table beside the sink. "You don't need that."

"I hadn't realized your resumé included work as a makeup artist," she said dryly.

"It doesn't. But having grown up with three sisters, I've picked up a few things. Besides, anytime you feel you need color in your cheeks, I'll be happy to oblige." He ducked his head and touched his mouth to hers in a light, unthreatening kiss.

As their lips met and clung for a brief, but unsettling moment, Grace felt her blood warm and her head begin to swim.

"There." Pulling back, he skimmed his knuckles up her cheekbones. "That's one helluva natural look you've got going there, darlin'."

Grace looked in the mirror, already knowing what she'd see. Her eyes were bright and slightly dazed, her cheeks flushed.

"This is insane," she muttered, embarrassed at the way he could so easily tangle her emotions.

"Absolutely crazy," he agreed with a cheerfulness that made her want to scream.

She wondered if her uncharacteristically rash behavior could possibly be another symptom of a breakdown. Contract negotiations always made her nervous; factor in Robert's lawsuit, and the threatening letters, and it would undoubtedly be surprising if she wasn't going a little crazy.

"You realize, of course, that your obnoxious, macho behavior is outrageously sexist. I'll bet you wouldn't be acting this way if I were a male writer."

"You're right. I've never felt an urge to kiss another guy." He skimmed his knuckles up her cheek again and enjoyed watching even more color bloom.

"I don't understand what's happening," she complained.

"We can discuss it later tonight. After you've done your duty. Meanwhile, since I'm experiencing this urge to indulge in more macho, sexist behavior, I suppose we'd better get downstairs."

"You're not going to kiss me again," she warned as they left the suite.

"Of course I am." He grinned, enjoying the way she tried so hard to pretend to be cool and composed when he'd already discovered her secret. "And you're going to love it."

Muttering a ripe curse, she picked up her pace, marching ahead of him toward the elevator.

Lucas enjoyed the sight of the soft feminine sway of her hips beneath that short silk, and tortured himself just a little by remembering how good she'd felt in his arms.

"Hey, Gracie," he called out as she punched the Down button with more force than necessary.

"What?" She refused to look at him.

"You really do have dynamite legs."

Taking her choked sound to be a muffled laugh, Lucas realized that when this conference was over, and Grace was safe—and he could not allow himself to believe otherwise—he was really going to have to call Samantha and thank her for dropping the gorgeous romance writer into his lap. And his life.

Although the two of them drew more than a few interested looks when they arrived in the Golden Gate Ballroom, Grace was relieved when none of the committee asked any questions about her tardiness. Then again, she thought, remembering her reflection in the bathroom mirror, they probably all knew exactly what she'd been doing. For some reason, that idea, which had seemed so disturbing upstairs, now actually struck her as rather appealing.

After the way Robert had so publicly dumped her, having everyone think that such a dashing macho hunk of a man could find her sexually attractive was proving a definite morale booster.

Which was the only reason, she assured herself, that she didn't complain when Marianne Tyler coaxed him into replacing a missing judge—an editor who'd apparently gotten food poisoning from the *Viva Italia* chicken salad on the flight from New York.

"It's really quite easy," Marianne assured him. "There are four categories. The first, and usually the most popular with the ladies, is the hunk contest, where you pick the man you'd most like to see on a book cover. The men are amateurs whose pictures are sent in by wives and girlfriends. And, occasionally, mothers."

Lucas tried to picture his mother sending in a near naked photograph of him and decided it would be easier to believe she'd been beamed aboard the mother ship by aliens. Now Fancy, he decided, was another story. He could almost imagine his unorthodox grandmother pulling a stunt like that.

"Then there's best character from a historical novel," Marianne was saying. "Along with the best from a contemporary, and the best from a paranormal–time travel."

"How am I supposed to know if the costumes are authentic?"

"Oh, don't worry about that," she said airily. "Just go with what strikes your fancy." That said, she bustled off with a rustle of silk.

"If I went with what struck my fancy," Lucas murmured to Grace, "I'd undoubtedly get us thrown out of here."

Grace wasn't about to touch that line. "I hadn't realized the two of you knew each other," she said instead. The way Marianne had been looking at him, undressing him with her eyes, for heaven's sake, had been very close to disgusting.

"We met earlier in the lobby. When I was looking for you. She thought I was her missing pirate."

"I'm not surprised." Grace sighed. "I was thinking the same thing," she admitted.

"Really?"

"Really. And before your ego gets entirely out of control, I have to clarify that I think it's your hair."

"I see." Uncaring of any audience they might have, he skimmed a knuckle up her cheek. "And here I was hoping it was my rakish good looks."

Grace told herself she should brush his hand away, but the truth was it felt too good. The deeper truth was that she was dying for him to touch her like that all over.

"Do you have any idea," he murmured, bending his head, his words meant for her ears only, "what it does to me when you look at me that way?"

She wasn't going to ask what way. Because she knew

that every thought, every desire, every wicked fantasy was undoubtedly written across her face in bold script. Before she could try to come up with an appropriate answer, a jarring male voice calling her name shattered the moment.

"Oh, no," she said with a moan.

"What's wrong?"

Later, Grace would realize the flash-fire change of mood, the way Lucas had gone from sexy and flirtatious to alert and strangely dangerous. Not emotionally dangerous as he'd been before; instead he'd suddenly become the man she'd gotten a fleeting glimpse of upstairs in the concierge lounge with Robert. A man capable of violence.

"It's Kevin."

"Kevin?" Lucas watched the hunk clad in a kilt like the one Alice Vail had suggested he wear striding toward the judges' table. "Is he a former lover?" Something that felt amazingly like jealousy clawed at his gut as he took in the almost pretty face and steely body obviously honed to perfection by hours of lifting weights in the gym.

"Kevin?" She laughed at that, but Lucas, who was watching and listening for every nuance, caught the nervousness in the faintly shaky sound. "Hardly. I told you, I gave up men after Robert."

He took her icy hand in his. "Until me."

"Please, Lucas." Her gaze was serious; her hand trembled. "I can handle only one troublesome male at a time."

He was about to ask what, exactly, was troublesome about a guy in a skirt, even one with arms like iron tree trunks, but before he had the chance, Kevin was standing in front of the table and solved the little mystery for him.

"Is it true?" he demanded of Grace.

"Is what true?" she hedged.

"I was talking with Geraldine Manning backstage. She

told me you've requested a different treatment for your next cover."

Grace sighed. She'd known she was going to have to face this problem, but hoped she could do it in her own way. In her own time.

She'd planned to speak to Kevin alone, somewhere quiet, where she could explain her reasoning and assure him how much she'd appreciated him posing for all her previous covers. But using her typical bull-in-a-china-shop approach, the publisher had escalated what Grace had known was going to be a sticky problem.

"It's nothing personal, Kevin." She tugged her hand free from Lucas's and placed it on Kevin's arm. When she felt the muscle tense like a boulder beneath her touch, she realized exactly how upset he was. "It's just that this next book is going to be my first without Robert—"

"All the more reason to have me on the cover," he countered. "Especially since everyone believes Robert was the one actually writing those bodice rippers."

"They're not bodice rippers," Lucas interjected mildly.

"What?" Kevin shot him a furious look.

"The term bodice rippers is outdated. And insulting," Lucas explained. "I'd think that you, working in the business as you do, should know that."

A dark angry color rose up Kevin's huge neck, suffusing his face like a fever. "I don't know who the hell you are, but just stay out of this. It's between Grace and me."

Turning away from Lucas, he bent forward, braced both hands on the table and leaned over Grace in a way meant to intimidate. "Do you think the people actually bought all those millions of books because of you? Or that obnoxious loser you were married to? They bought the books because I was on the cover."

Grace stared at his face, which was no longer cover-model handsome, but ugly, twisted with a hatred he didn't bother to conceal. "I made Roberta Grace," he almost growled. "Dump me and you'll be sorry."

"If you don't get away from this table now," Lucas said in that same, quiet spooky voice Grace had heard him use with Robert, "you'll be looking for a new occupation. Because unless someone writes a romance about a guy with every bone in his face and body broken, you're going to have a hard time getting your picture on any more covers."

Grace watched the awareness rise in Kevin's eyes, and could tell the exact moment when he realized that Lucas's warning was not an idle threat.

He straightened, his hands clenched into fists at his sides.

"You'll be sorry," he repeated. Then, as Robert had done before him when faced with Lucas's coldly murderous gaze, he marched away.

He was not the only one who'd been frightened. Grace swallowed past the lump in her throat. "We have to talk about your propensity to threaten to beat people up."

"Not just any people," he clarified. "Men who threaten you."

Terrific, Lucas mentally blasted himself. In trying to protect Grace, he'd succeeded in frightening her instead. This was definitely not the feeling he wanted her to have toward him.

"There you are," a voice behind them proclaimed on a distinctly British accent, forestalling any attempt at an explanation Lucas might have been planning. "I've been searching the hotel for you two."

"We sure seem to be popular," Lucas muttered to Grace. Tamping down his frustration, he turned and watched a woman approaching in long, self-assured strides, rather like a steamer coming into port. She was tall with a firm body, good bones that spoke of pedigree, and prematurely silver hair that had been styled in a sleek cut to show off her high cheekbones. Her suit was black, obviously expensive and tailored to fit perfectly. If she'd been a few years younger—Lucas guessed her age to be somewhere in her forties—she could have easily been a runway model.

Following in her wake was a short, egg-shaped man with thinning hair and round, metal-framed spectacles. Lucas figured him to be in his early to middle thirties. He was wearing a brown suit and a bow tie and carrying a fluffy white dog. The dog was decked out in red taffeta.

"Grace, I'm so pleased to see you've finally left your hermitage." Geraldine Manning greeted her with a kiss on the cheek. "How nice you've deigned to grace us all with your presence. No pun intended," she said with a merry laugh.

Before Grace could answer, she'd turned her attention to Lucas and held out a manicured hand. "I'm Geraldine Manning, the new publisher of Penbrook Press."

"Pleased to meet you, ma'am," Lucas said as he shook the outstretched hand. He was not surprised when her grip proved firm and confident. "I'm Lucas Kincaid."

"Call me Geraldine. Ma'am makes me feel ancient. You must be the man everyone's been buzzing about. I'd heard that Grace's escort was dashing, but I'd never expected you to look as if you'd just stepped out of one of her books." She glanced back toward Grace. "Aren't you currently working on a pirate book, Grace, dear?"

"That's right." Grace was moderately surprised, with all Geraldine had on her plate these days, that she was aware of her latest proposal. "Set in the Caribbean," she added absently, trying her best not to stare at the dog.

The publisher skimmed another look over Lucas. "Well, you shouldn't run out of inspiration. Should she, George?" she asked the other man.

"I shouldn't think so," he agreed.

"Grace, Lucas, this is George Dwyer, editorial director of Penbrook Press. Be nice to him, Grace," she suggested with a wink, "he's not only the heir to the empire, he's directly responsible for Rainbow Romances. Perhaps you can base one of your heroes on him. You'd like that, wouldn't you, Georgie?"

Her deep laugh boomed out, causing the dog to leap out of the editorial director's arms. He took off after it as it made a beeline for the door, red taffeta trailing on the floor.

"Oh dear. Dalai is a bit nervous tonight," Geraldine said with a slight sigh as they watched the small dog effectively dodging George Dwyer's desperate lunges. "I believe she must still be a bit airsick from the turbulence our flight ran into over the Rockies."

"Her name is Dolly?" Grace asked, trying to be polite.

"Dalai. As in the Dalai Lama. She's a Lhasa apso. They're from Tibet, of course, so the name seemed to fit."

"Cute costume," Lucas offered.

"It's a copy of the dress Bette Davis wore in *Jezebel*. Dalai and I love to curl up in bed and watch those old movies together."

"It must be nice having a pet," Grace said. Her mother had always found a dog or cat to be too much trouble. Robert, unsurprisingly, was against her bringing anything into the house that might deflect attention from him.

"Oh, Dalai isn't a pet, darling. She's a member of the family. Like a daughter." The sound of cymbals crashing drew her attention to the orchestra pit, where Dalai was now trying to take refuge. "Sometimes, admittedly, she's a bit of a naughty daughter."

She shook her head. "I'd best go help George. Heaven knows, he and Dalai have never hit it off. I keep telling him that he's trying too hard, that dogs can sense insecurity, but the poor boy doesn't seem to listen."

She paused before leaving and gave Lucas one more long, judicious look. "You really are magnificent. I don't suppose you've ever thought of becoming a model?"

"No, ma'am," Lucas said quickly.

"That's too bad. Because with you on the covers, Rainbow Romances would fly off the shelves." She took a business card from her evening bag and held it out to him. "Just in case you're ever in the mood for a career change."

"I'll keep that in mind." He put the card in his shirt pocket and ignored Grace's teasing grin.

"I don't want to hear a single word," he warned when they were alone again.

"I'm not going to say a thing," she promised, smothering a giggle.

"Thank you. I appreciate that, darlin'." Lucas rubbed his chin as he watched the couple trying to cut the dog off at the foot of the stage. "Old Georgie doesn't exactly look like the heir to a publishing fortune, does he? More flunky than scion."

"I was thinking the same thing. And I'm not certain how much he knows about publishing, since up until his father bought Penbrook Press, which also publishes Rainbow Romances, he'd been working in the diaper-design department."

"The diaper-design department?"

"Of Dwyer's Drier Diapers. If he's going to be the new editorial director, I may have to consider leaving Penbrook." She sighed. Yet one more problem she didn't need right now. "Although, to give him credit, he *is* the one who came up with the environmentally friendly 'green' disposable diaper that self-destructs in landfills."

"That's admirable. But I can't see what it has to do with publishing."

"My point, exactly."

"So you're thinking of switching houses?" he asked casually.

"The buyout has changed Penbrook. And so far, not for the better. Tina thinks I should move on. But I've had a good relationship with the company and would really prefer to stay. If we can work things out."

"There's something to be said for dancing with them that brung you," he agreed, quoting the folksy axiom he'd heard innumerable times growing up.

"True, but…" She sighed. "It's complicated."

Before he could dig a little deeper, there was a fanfare from the orchestra pit. A moment later, the red-carpeted runway filled with men and women dressed in a fantasy realm of costuming that pushed the boundaries of imagination while dazzling the senses.

There were enough beads and sequins to have made several villages of women in India go blind from the handiwork, and Grace was certain the number of feathers adorning the various outfits would have given any bird-loving Audubon Society member a heart attack. Hair and makeup were as theatrical as any Las Vegas or Atlantic City revue. Unsurprisingly, if the applause, wolf whistles and suggestive female shouts at the wannabe cover-model hunks were any indication, the audience was already loving the show.

After the parade came a lavish song-and-dance number. Then the introduction of the judges by the master of ceremonies, a popular game show host who'd won fame and fortune by setting up blind dates, then sending a camera along to capture every—hopefully—embarrassing moment.

The judges were an eclectic mix. Along with Grace and

Lucas, there was an eccentric painter renowned for his romance novel covers—and infamous for his torrid affairs with several of the models, who were young enough to be his granddaughters. There was a representative from a California vineyard specializing in sparkling wine, a former Miss America, and Geraldine Manning, making her first appearance as publisher of Penbrook Press and, of course, the M.C. pointed out, as publisher of Rainbow Romances.

Because of the seating arrangement, Grace was the next-to-last judge to be introduced, right before Lucas. As she heard herself called "one-half—the better half—of Roberta Grace," she pasted a professional smile on her face, stood up and faced the fans, whose enthusiastic applause almost made this very public appearance worthwhile.

After a brief introduction of Lucas, the first competition, the cover-model contest, began, to the driving beat of the Village People's old hit, "Macho Man." The parade of near naked male flesh had the women going wild, as Indians, cowboys, pirates, Scots Highlanders, warriors, knights and outlaws strutted their stuff for the crowd. One masked man was twirling his six-shooters, firing blanks up at the ceiling.

Over the driving disco beat, Grace thought she heard the sound of wood splintering just above her head. Before she could react, she was thrown to the ground and Lucas was lying on top of her.

6

FIFTEEN MINUTES LATER, Grace was back in her suite with Lucas. But they were not alone. Geraldine, George, Tina and Jamie, along with two San Francisco detectives who'd shown up after Lucas had called the shooting in to the police, were also there.

Shooting. The word continued to reverberate in her head like the gunfire that had splintered that nearby pillar. Someone had actually tried to kill her. Or at least frighten her to death, which, if that had been her assailant's intention, he'd almost succeeded in doing.

"Hey, Kincaid." A tall man with a lantern jaw and pewter crewcut, who'd introduced himself as Detective Robert MacDonald, greeted Lucas. "I thought you'd quit the bodyguard business."

"I was planning to." Lucas glanced over at Grace, who was curled into a corner of the ivory brocade sofa, holding the cup of tea Geraldine had ordered from room service. "But something came up." Although his words were directed at the detective, he didn't take his gaze from Grace. "Samantha was in a bind. She needed me to do this one last job."

"Grace," Tina asked, "is this true? You actually hired a bodyguard?"

"It seemed like a good idea at the time." The teacup rattled as Grace lowered it to the gilt-rimmed saucer.

Although she'd made a feeble protest when Lucas had scooped her up from the carpeting, held her against his chest and carried her through the excited throng to the elevator, truthfully, she'd been relieved, since she hadn't been all that sure that her legs, which were shaking like the rest of her, would have been capable of holding her up.

"I don't understand," Geraldine complained. When she took a cigarette out of her bag, George jumped up to light it. "Why on earth would you hire a bodyguard? Not that he's not lovely to look at," she amended. Then, realizing that was perhaps not the most politically correct thing to say, she glanced over at Lucas. "No offense intended, darling."

"None taken," Lucas agreed easily.

"It's a bit complicated," Grace said. "I've been getting these letters—"

"The people in the mail room tell me you receive the most fan mail of any of our writers. Even more than the mystery author who writes the whodunits featuring the lesbian black medical examiner."

"Well, these aren't exactly fan letters."

"They're threats," Tina revealed flatly.

"Threats?" George asked, his eyes going wide behind the thick lenses of his glasses. "As in death threats?"

"That's right. And although I'm a little miffed that Grace didn't see fit to reveal Mr. Kincaid's true reason for being at the conference, I, for one, am grateful he was here," Tina continued.

"I agree," Jamie said, bestowing a warm look on the subject of their discussion. "After all, who knows what might have happened if Lucas hadn't been with Grace this evening?"

Vaguely remembering hearing a second shot as she'd been pinioned beneath him, Grace had been thinking much the same thing.

"You're right, of course," Geraldine said from a cloud

of blue smoke. "But I'm still stunned that you've been going through all this, Grace, and didn't tell us."

"I wasn't overly concerned until another letter was waiting for me here at the hotel," Grace admitted. "Since I'd seen this classified advertisement, I called the agency on a whim."

"You found a bodyguard in the classifieds?" Tina asked the same question Jamie had asked earlier.

"Actually, as impossible as it sounds, I did."

"Are you any good?" Geraldine asked Lucas.

"He was good enough to save my life." Grace spoke up, earning a faint smile from the man whose body she imagined she could still feel against her own.

"That could have been a fluke," George volunteered.

"I doubt that," the second detective said. "S. J. Slade runs a first-class private protection agency. And Kincaid's one of her top operatives."

"Even so, there are so many people at the conference, it seems as if it's going to be impossible to keep whoever fired that shot from trying again," Tina said with a frown. "Perhaps you should just cancel your participation, Grace," she suggested. "No one would blame you for going home."

"And leave Robert to accept my ROMI if I win?" Grace folded her arms. "Not in this lifetime. I refuse to cave in and surrender just because some crazed reader appears to have gone off the deep end."

"Well, now that we have that settled," MacDonald said, with ill-concealed impatience, "perhaps you can fill me in on these letters, Ms. Fairchild. There's a very good chance that a would-be murderer is still in the hotel. And I'd like to begin my investigation sometime in this century."

"I'm sorry." The gritty suggestion that her would-be

assassin might be lurking somewhere close by chilled Grace's blood again.

"I've received four over the past two months. The latest was waiting for me when I arrived at the hotel this morning."

"Obviously it's someone who knew you were going to be here."

It was the same thing that Lucas had suggested earlier in the bar. Grace gave him the same answer.

"Terrific." The detective rubbed his jaw. "Advance publicity and two thousand potential suspects."

Not having an answer for that, Grace stood up, went into the bedroom and returned with the slender stack of envelopes.

A silence settled over the room as he turned his attention to the letters, then passed them on to the other detective.

There was more questioning. Although Grace was definitely uncomfortable discussing personal problems, she related the facts of her divorce, since she knew that Lucas would tell if she didn't. As well as her threats from Kevin.

"So, who all knew about these letters?"

"Jamie," Grace said, wishing she hadn't involved her best friend in such an unsavory situation. "And Tina. And, of course, I told Lucas—Mr. Kincaid—this afternoon."

"That's all?"

"Yes."

MacDonald turned to Tina. "If you don't mind, ma'am, I'd like to ask you a few questions. And you, too, Ms. Manning."

"Of course," Tina said.

"Anything I can do to help," Geraldine said. She stabbed her cigarette out in a crystal ashtray etched with the crown logo of the hotel, then promptly lit another one.

Although both women consented without hesitation, Lucas noticed that neither of them appeared overly thrilled by the circumstances, either. He got the feeling that rather than appearing concerned for Grace, they were mostly peeved at having been dragged into the investigation.

Eventually, everyone left and Grace once again found herself alone with Lucas. Fortunately, after the adrenaline burst that had come with being shot at had faded away, she'd been left with an exhaustion that almost—but not entirely—overcame her attraction to him.

"How are you holding up?" He was sitting across from her, sprawled out in a wing chair in a way that reminded her of a lazy lion. But from the speed with which he'd thrown her to the floor, Grace knew looks were decidedly deceptive.

"I'm fine. Thanks to you." She gripped her hands together to keep them from trembling. "You saved my life." It was still a stunning thought—not so much that Lucas had protected her, but that someone had attempted to kill her in the first place.

She leaned her head against the back of the sofa, closed her eyes and began massaging her temples, where the headache that had threatened earlier was now throbbing.

"I was just doing my job."

It took an effort, but she opened her eyes. "Is that all it was?"

"What do you think?"

"That's just the problem. I don't know what to think about any of this."

"It's going to be all right, Gracie. You're going to be all right." He got up from the chair and came around behind her, replacing her fingers with his larger, callused ones.

"I believe you're going to keep me safe." His touch was so extraordinarily tender. "But there's more going on here. You have to understand, after Robert I swore that I wasn't going to let myself get involved again. Not that we're involved," she said hastily. "I mean, not really, but—"

"Of course we are." His hands moved to her braid, unweaving it so his fingers could massage the back of her head, the nape of her neck. "Just because neither one of us were looking for this doesn't mean we can deny it, either." His palms moved to her tensed shoulders as he began working out the knots.

"It's only chemistry," she murmured. His clever, soothing touch made her want to purr. "Sex."

"Don't knock chemistry. It's what makes diamonds different from coal. Gold from brass. Some of the most potent physical reactions in the universe are the results of chemistry." Drawn by the scent of her hair, which reminded him of summer sunshine and ocean breezes, he kissed the top of her head. "And since you brought it up, sugar, I've never been one to discount sex."

"I'll just bet you haven't."

"It's different with you." He brushed her hair aside and touched his lips to her neck, in that surprisingly sensitive little hollow right behind her ear he'd discovered earlier. "This morning I'd quit my job and was on my way to Alaska."

"What's in Alaska?"

"Whales. Jagged, snow-capped peaks shimmering with glaciers thrusting upward into an unbelievably blue sky. Grizzlies. Wolves. And scenery so wild and unspoiled it'll take your breath away."

"What are you going to do there?"

"Sail. Soak up the sights. Play. Want to come with me, Gracie?"

Her life had been so centered around work these past years, she couldn't remember the last time she'd played.

And it had been even longer still since she'd skimmed across the waves with the sea breeze blowing in her hair and the spray of saltwater on her face. It sounded heavenly. And impossible.

"I don't think so. I have books to write—"

"You can write them in Alaska." His lips skimmed down her neck, leaving a sparkling trail of flames. "The scenery and the solitude will inspire your creativity."

"It sounds lovely."

"Better than lovely. It'll be an adventure. Just think of it, sugar, you and I in Alaska, sailing along the empty miles of coastline, exploring hidden inlets, diving overboard to swim naked in the sea—"

"We'd freeze."

"Nah." His hands moved over her shoulder and down her arms. "I promise, I'll keep you plenty warm enough."

Of that Grace had not a single doubt. "I have responsibilities."

"Screw them." The suggestion rumbled in her ear even as it tried to take root in her heart. "So far, in the last few hours, I've met your rat ex-husband, your agent, your publisher and a hunk of a cover model who's ticked off at you because you decided to dump the clinch covers. From what I can see, there are an awful lot of people sitting back getting a piece of the action."

"It's not like that." She pulled out of his arms, turned around and went up on her knees on the couch so she could look him directly in the eye. "What you see as exploitation, I see as teamwork. Except for Robert," she explained. "We all have one goal in mind, to put out the best story we can."

"And what if one of the team members is trying to kill you?"

"Surely you don't suspect Geraldine or Tina?"

"Right now I suspect everyone who was in that room tonight. And so should you."

"I can't live that way." She squeezed her eyes shut. When she opened them again, Lucas still reminded her of one of her heroes. But not a pirate. His rugged face had turned gladiator grim. "Not trusting anyone."

"That hunk in the plaid skirt threatened you."

"Kilt. And Kevin's always had a terrible temper. Since his picture sells books, people put up with it."

"You're also cutting off your ex's gravy train."

"True. But believe me, Lucas, it would take more guts than Robert could possess in several lifetimes for him to risk a murder attempt."

"Maybe himself. But he could have hired that fake outlaw. The masked man who appears to have ridden off into the sunset without anyone knowing who he was. Or how he ended up in the pageant without an entry form."

"Do we have to talk about this now?" she complained. The headache was trying to return. "I'm going to have nightmares as it is."

"Okay." Lucas reluctantly reminded himself that it was technically MacDonald's job to find the shooter. "So, going back to my offer of an all-expenses-paid vacation to paradise, when was the last time you strolled along a beach and watched the sun set into the sea?"

"I live in New York. It rises out of the sea on the East Coast."

"Sounds as if you're due for a change."

Grace didn't know whether to laugh at his tenacity or cry. The smothered sound she managed was a bit of both. "Are you always this stubborn?"

"When I want something, absolutely."

"And you want me."

"More than I've ever wanted any woman in my life."

Grace made her living with words. She'd certainly

written similar dialogue for characters innumerable times before. But never had any pretty words of love spoken by any man—real or imaginary—possessed the power of that single, tersely uttered declaration.

"You're going to think I'm a hysterical female—"

"Not hysterical." But definitely female, he decided, as those glorious breasts rose and fell with her deep breath.

"That's funny. Since I feel on the verge of a nervous breakdown right now. And, although I hate to admit it, and I know I said I didn't want to talk about what happened, or your reason for being here, I'm scared...."

Her voice deserted her. Repressing a shudder, Grace pressed her lips together, determined to regain control. "Oh, God." She covered her eyes and hated how she felt. Frightened, fragile, needy.

He wanted to hold her, but knowing that would lead to kissing her, which could all-too-easily lead to something else, Lucas reminded himself that he'd been brought up to believe in an old-fashioned chivalry that had ironclad rules about taking advantage of vulnerable women.

"I know just what you need."

"What?" she mumbled from behind her hands.

"Bed."

"What?" Embarrassed by her crumbling composure, but surprised by his quiet, matter-of-fact statement, Grace forced herself to look up at him.

"You need to get to bed." He smiled as he came around to stand in front of the sofa. "And, although it's definitely not my first choice, alone."

"Are you leaving?"

Although she hated revealing weakness, Grace knew that she wouldn't get any sleep at all if she were by herself listening for every little sound, waiting for that outlaw assassin to break into her room and kill her.

Murder. The idea, in the abstract, was unpalatable. The

thought of herself as a murder victim was incomprehensible.

"Not on a bet. I'd stay even if I wasn't getting paid, Gracie. Because when that guy took a potshot at you tonight, he made things personal. Real personal."

When his voice threatened to choke up at the memory of how close that shooter had come to succeeding, Lucas swallowed in an attempt to wash away the acrid taste of fury.

"And since it's obvious that you're dead on your feet, although I wanted to get you out of the hotel tonight to someplace safer, we'll save that until morning."

"I can't leave tomorrow morning. I'm scheduled to give the keynote speech."

"Cancel it."

She might give in to him on protection matters. She might even allow herself to be tempted, just a little, by the idea of running away from her responsibilities and going to Alaska. But there was no way Grace was going to allow Lucas to dictate to her regarding her career decisions.

"I can't. No," she amended with a toss of her head. "What I meant to say was that I won't."

She was trying to come up with the best way to try to explain the importance of this speech, not only to announce her solo career in this most public of forums, but to prove to herself that she didn't need Robert—or anyone else—to handle her career for her, when, once again, Lucas surprised her.

"Okay. If it's that important to you, we'll work something out."

"Thank you." She might not be willing to permit anyone to take over her new, independent life, but she wasn't foolish enough not to accept help when it was offered. "That's very understanding of you."

"I've been known to have my moments." He held out

his hand, and as she took it, his look turned serious. "I'm not Robert, Gracie. Not in any way."

"I know." Any comparison between the two men would be ludicrous.

"Tomorrow we'll talk. About Alaska." Lucas found himself wishing that they'd met in any other way. That he could forget about the need to protect her life and concentrate on ways to win her heart. But life, he'd found, was seldom simple.

"I can't go to Alaska."

"Hawaii then." The idea of Grace in a bikini was definitely appealing. "Think of it, Gracie—a land of tropical flowers so bright they almost blind you, lush green valleys, volcanoes, sand that sparkles like black diamonds. And all along the coast are hidden coves where we can get naked and swim in the blue-green waters—"

"Do all your fantasies involve getting wet and naked?"

"Of course not. Want to hear the one about how I've rescued you from an avalanche, and I carry you miles through the knee-deep snow until we get to a cabin, where, after we stumble in, I light a fire and—"

"We get naked."

"Of course. Because our clothes are all wet from the snow."

He'd linked their fingers together as he walked her the few feet to the bedroom door, and for the moment Grace allowed herself to pretend that this evening had never happened, that the shooter hadn't existed, that Lucas was not her bodyguard, but merely a man who was walking her home after a pleasant date. A date that held the promise of more to come.

"I knew it. Wet and naked. Admit it, Lucas. Your fantasies are stuck in a rut."

He laughed at that. "I guess you're right. And you can call me a sexist pig, darlin', but I can't imagine how any red-blooded male could spend two minutes with you and not experience the same fantasy."

"Since I'm not up to giving a lecture on sexist comments, I believe I'll just take that as a compliment," she decided.

"You do that. Because it's the truth. Want to hear a few more of my more colorful fantasies?"

"Perhaps tomorrow." Fatigue had returned, fogging her head and weakening her body and her resolve. If she didn't get away from him now, Grace was afraid she'd end up inviting him to bed with her.

"Definitely tomorrow."

Lucas nearly groaned as he read the sensual thoughts that were turning her eyes back to that sexy shade of green. Did the woman have any idea what she did to him when she looked at him that way? Did she realize that he was about two seconds from dragging her off to bed and doing what they both obviously wanted?

Although it was torture, Lucas slipped his hands into his pockets, because he didn't trust himself to touch her again. "Say good-night, Gracie."

She gave him a look of gratitude for having once again saved her—this time from herself. "Good night, Lucas."

Grace went into the bedroom and shut the door behind her. It took her less than two minutes to wash her face and brush her teeth. She took her Marge Simpson nightshirt from the suitcase she still hadn't finished unpacking, pulled it over her head and collapsed into bed. And although she wouldn't have thought it possible, given all she'd been through in the past few hours, she fell instantly to sleep.

While Grace slept in the neighboring room, Lucas lay on the too-short sofa, looking out at the city lights and, in the distance, the bridge all ablaze with lights, and wondered idly how long it would take Gracie and him to melt every glacier in Alaska.

IF GRACE WAS CONCERNED about being alone in her suite with Lucas the next morning, she need not have worried. Because when she left the bedroom after her shower, fully dressed with makeup on, she found them all back in the living room, waiting for her. Dalai was there as well, claiming the best chair, dressed today in a black leather Harley jacket and cap that made her look like a biker mop.

"I hadn't realized the conference had been moved to my suite," Grace said dryly.

"We're not going to let you go downstairs alone," Tina said. "Not after what happened last night."

"Gee, I never realized that your agenting responsibility included throwing yourself in the way of a bullet for your writer," Grace said mildly. "I would have guessed such sacrifice would have required at least a twenty-percent commission."

"You know we're all concerned about you, Grace."

"I've never doubted that, Tina. Not even when I saw you and Robert having that little tête-à-tête in the hallway before the pageant last night."

The agent's face paled only slightly, but Lucas, who was watching the exchange carefully, noticed her body stiffen and her eyes dart nervously toward Geraldine Manning, who was watching the exchange with interest.

"He wanted to speak with me. What was I to do?" Tina seemed to be asking the room in general. "If I'd refused and tried to walk away, he might have made a scene. And that certainly wouldn't have helped the image rebuilding we're supposed to be doing at this conference."

"Image rebuilding?" Grace's tone was still tightly controlled.

Her temper, Lucas noted with interest, was less so. Her remarkable eyes flashed that green he was accustomed to seeing when he kissed her. Oh yes, he thought with satisfaction, Grace Fairfield was definitely a woman of strong passions. She was like a volcano simmering beneath an arctic glacier, and he, for one, was definitely looking forward to being there when all that ice melted.

"I hadn't realized my image needed an overhaul."

"That's because you've never had to think about those things," the agent countered. "You've just written your books, while Robert and I were out busting our butts to sell them to publishers and the public."

"I see." Her eyes were frost. Icicles were now dripping from her words. Lucas was fascinated by the transformation to ice queen. "How fortunate I had the two of you to do all that for me. Allowing me to live in my little romantic fantasy world—"

"Gracie," he interrupted smoothly, "would you like a cup of coffee? Or tea?"

Realizing that her control was becoming ragged at the edges, Grace managed a grateful smile at him for having come to her rescue. "Coffee sounds terrific."

"You've got it." He poured the coffee from a silver pot. As he placed it onto the mahogany butler's table in front of the sofa, she caught a glimpse of his shoulder holster and felt a now-familiar chill skim over her.

"And you've got to taste these cinnamon rolls," Jamie insisted. She put one on a gilt-rimmed porcelain plate, then placed the plate on the table beside the cup. "They're simply scrumptious."

The spicy, tantalizing scent wafted upward. "I'm on a diet," Grace demurred.

"Oh, that's ridiculous," Jamie argued. "You look marvelous just the way you are. Besides, men prefer women with curves. It gives them something to hold on to in bed. Isn't that true, Lucas?"

"Works for me," he agreed with a bold grin as he took in those voluptuous curves in question. Today's suit was a tailored navy blue with white trim. Her blouse was white silk and fastened with pearl buttons that had him thinking about her milkmaid's skin.

When she sat down and crossed her legs with a swish of silk, Lucas felt an urge to touch her, just a skim of a fingertip along a smooth thigh.

Grace took a sip of the French roast coffee and drank in the sight of Lucas, who'd reclaimed the wing chair.

He was conservatively dressed again this morning, in gray slacks, a blue shirt, navy blazer and tie, but his dark hair, which was tied back again at the nape of his neck, along with that crescent-shaped scar on his cheek, gave an underlying impression of mystery and danger. One she found all too intriguing.

Afraid he might pick up on her thoughts, Grace turned her attention to the plate Jamie had placed in front of her. The scent was nearly as seductive as Lucas's kisses.

Enticed, she took a bite. And practically swooned as flavors and textures flowed across her tongue, stimulating all her taste buds. "Oh, this is delicious." She nearly moaned with pleasure. As she took another melt-in-the-mouth bite, Grace decided that the sweet roll undoubtedly contained enough sugar and fat to have the food police ban it for life.

The caffeine from the coffee began to kick in, blowing away the foggy remnants of the dreams, clearing her mind. Grace was licking the white frosting from her fingers when Geraldine Manning decided to enter the discussion.

"I don't want to sound as if I'm taking sides, Grace," she said, more carefully than her usual rapid-fire approach to conversation. "But Tina does have a point." She took a cigarette from the pack in her purse. As he'd done last night, George leaped forward to light it.

"Romance publishing isn't about romance. It's about the bottom line. And, unfortunately, image plays a part in a writer's popularity. For years everyone has assumed that Robert was the one actually writing the Roberta Grace books—"

"Everyone?"

"Well, perhaps not *everyone*." The publisher back-tracked a bit. "But it's certainly the prevailing opinion."

"That was my mistake." Grace frowned and ran her finger around the gold rim of the cup. "One I have every intention of correcting. Beginning today." Her tone was stiff. Her shoulders, Lucas noticed, were even stiffer. He decided it was time to end this conversation.

"I'd like to spend a few minutes with Ms. Fairfield going over today's agenda," he said. "Why don't the rest of you go on ahead? It won't take long."

Appearing more than happy to leave Grace and Lucas alone, Jamie jumped up immediately. Although Grace had a suspicion that Tina and Geraldine weren't all that eager to leave, Lucas deftly and politely hustled them from the suite. Just before the door closed behind them, she heard Jamie cheerfully admiring Dalai's dominatrix costume.

"Oh, I would have loved to have heard Geraldine's answer to that one," Grace murmured.

Lucas laughed. A little pool of silence settled over them.

"You're carrying a gun," she said finally.

"Never leave home without it."

"Are you expecting to shoot someone today?"

"I'd just as soon not."

"But you will. If you have to."

"In a heartbeat."

Grace thought about that. "That detective was right. You are very good at your job."

"You've come to that decision because I'm carrying?"

"No. It was your eyes."

He arched a dark brow. "My eyes?"

"They seem calm most of the time, almost lazy. But they're taking in everything. I was watching you watching Tina and Geraldine, and it was almost as if I could see the continual click of a mental camera shutter."

"Very good." He lifted his cup of cold coffee in a salute. "You're very observant."

"I'm a writer. It comes with the territory. Sort of like carrying guns comes with being a bodyguard."

A bodyguard. On a distant level, she was still waiting to wake up and discover that she'd dreamed this entire frightening scenario. As mental pictures of last night's shooting came crashing to the front of her mind again, Grace closed her eyes.

"I'm sorry," she murmured. "I just need a minute."

"Take your time." Because he couldn't refrain from touching another second, Lucas lifted her off the sofa, gathered her into his arms and ran his hand over the smooth crown of her hair.

She'd pulled it back into that tidy, efficient knot again today, but Lucas could remember all too well how seductive she'd looked last night, with it swirling loose around her shoulders like a tawny cloud, her eyes wide with passion.

"I don't have any time." She rested her forehead against his chest. "I'm due downstairs and we still haven't gotten around to discussing our agenda."

"Don't worry about it." His palms moved down her neck, his fingers soothing out knotted muscles as he had last night. "I just used that as an excuse to clear everyone out. I could tell you were getting tense, and I figured, since I'd been put in charge of taking care of your body, that the least I could do is send you downstairs feeling relaxed and loose."

His touch was heaven. It was agony. It also made her knees weak in that now familiar way. But it still wasn't enough.

Lucas made her feel things she'd never felt before. He fascinated her; he made her want to toss caution to the four winds, throw herself into his arms and discover firsthand the passion his eyes, his lips, his touch promised. But most of all, she wanted him to help her forget that her life was in danger.

"I can think of a better way to relax me."

His smile was slow, seductive and pleased. "Oh darlin'," he murmured as he caught her chin between his fingers. "I thought you'd never ask."

When his lips touched hers, Grace slid her arms beneath his blazer, excited by the ripple of muscle beneath her splayed fingers. Passion rose quickly, as it always seemed to do with Lucas.

"I need to touch you." His words were ripped from his throat with a groan as he reached beneath her jacket and tugged her white silk blouse free of her waistband.

"Yes." She was racing into a smoky world. "Oh, please." She heard the rasp of callused flesh against silk, felt her breasts swell painfully beneath his palms, then gasped in pleasure as a roughened fingertip scraped against a tingling nipple.

Grace had never known she could feel so much. She clung to him desperately, her avid hands moving fretfully over his back. When her stroking hand touched the strap of his shoulder holster, a panicky reality came crashing down on her like a torrent of icy water, drowning the flames.

"It's okay," he soothed, when he felt her heart stutter beneath his palm. Felt her body tense and her satiny flesh turn cold and pebbly.

Frustrated and aching, and angry at himself for not having realized that Grace might not find the idea of a pistol conducive to seduction, Lucas retrieved his hands and willed his mind to something as close to sanity as he could manage while his body continued to throb painfully.

Timing, he thought wryly, was everything.

"Don't be afraid." He cupped her cheek, his warm gaze meant to reassure. "I promise not to let anyone hurt you, Grace." He bent his head again and brushed his lips against hers. "You have to trust me."

"I do." The words wafted on a shivery sigh from her lips to his. In contrast to the violence the gun and holster represented, his lips were heartbreakingly tender.

Grace trusted Lucas to protect her from whoever had written her those letters. Whoever, as impossible as it seemed, might want to kill her. She did worry about who was going to protect her from him, and even more to the point, from herself and her own unruly yearnings.

"If I don't get downstairs right away, they'll all undoubtedly come back up here to check and make certain I haven't been murdered." She sighed again. "I'm surprised Geraldine didn't have you take the hair dryer out of the bathroom so I couldn't accidentally electrocute myself in the bathtub."

"Good point." He pulled a small tape recorder out of his jacket pocket and clicked it on. "Note to yourself. More accidents happen in the bathroom than any other room. In the interest of protection, you should not let Gracie bathe alone."

Her answering laugh expelled the rest of her tension. "You really are incorrigible."

"That's what my grandma Fancy always used to say. Right before she'd drag me out to the woodshed." He put a hand out, silently advising Grace to wait until he'd checked out the hallway. "All clear."

Grace tried to imagine anyone dragging this man anywhere he didn't want to go, and failed. "Your grandmother must be a formidable woman."

"Oh, she is. Her people are from the Scottish Highlands. All wild folk. Their blood flows in her veins. All us Kincaids are terrified of Fancy. She might not be any bigger than a New York minute, but she can wield a willow switch with the best of them."

Grace wondered what it was about Lucas that he could make her crazy one minute, then turn around and have her feeling so relaxed and comfortable with him the next.

"That's something I would probably pay to see."

"I'm getting the feeling that despite your cream puff exterior, you can be a cruel-hearted woman from time to time, Gracie." He grinned down at her. "Fancy's going to love you."

Grace thought again what a contradiction this man seemed to be. On the one hand he was capable of shooting another person, but on the other, he seemed to have no trouble professing love and affection for his family. His colorful grandmother, in particular.

Grace also decided it was too bad that once the conference was over and Lucas was on his way to Alaska and she to New York, it was unlikely Fancy Kincaid and she would ever meet.

7

"OH, NO." They'd no sooner exited the elevator than
Grace saw a woman clad in a pink silk suit trimmed in
black marching toward her. The jacket strained over high
firm breasts that Grace knew were the result of last year's
"fluffing up."

"Grace, darling!" She went up on the toes of her sky-
scraper stiletto sandals and kissed Grace's cheek, envel-
oping her in a suffocating cloud of patchouli. "I've been
frantic ever since I heard about your near death experience." Her voice was thick with a Southern accent Lucas
recognized right away as feigned.

"I wouldn't exactly say near death," Grace murmured.

"That's our Grace." The smile curving the woman's
glossy, rose-tinted lips did not quite reach her hard blue
eyes. "Always so understated. If anyone ever shot at me,
why, I'd have to take to my bed for a week." She pressed
a manicured hand against her silicone enhanced chest as
she looked up at Lucas. "You must be the bodyguard."

He exchanged a quick glance with Grace, who rolled
her eyes, as if suggesting this was what she'd been afraid
of all along.

"Lucas, this is Anne Kilgallen."

"The Queen of Romance," the woman elaborated as
she smiled up at him.

"Anne, this is Lucas Kincaid. And he's not a bodyguard. He's an old friend—"

"Oh, I know, darling, I've heard that story. And of

course we all know that's exactly what it is. A story. To try to keep this horrible threat against your life hushed up." She placed a hand on Lucas's sleeve. "Don't worry." Her voice lowered intimately. "I promise not to breathe a word to anyone."

"That's very considerate of you, ma'am." Lucas smiled blandly as her pink-tipped fingers stroked his arm. "But I'm afraid you're mistaken—"

"Oh, really," she said with a trill of a laugh Grace suspected she'd spent years perfecting, "you two may as well drop the charade. Since no one is going to believe it. After all," she said, derision sharpening the saccharine magnolia tones, "Mr. Kincaid isn't the type of man a woman like you would be involved with. No offense intended, darling."

"None taken," Grace replied, her smile as fake as her adversary's. "How are you doing? Do you have a book out?" It was petty to ask, since now that she thought of it, Grace realized she hadn't seen a new novel from the writer in three years. But after that crack about her inability to attract a man like Lucas, she couldn't resist.

"Not at the moment. I've been in the process of changing agents. And publishers. As a matter of fact," she said, sotto voce, as if sharing a deep dark secret, "Geraldine Manning has been courting me to come over to Penbrook. If I've told her once, I've told her a thousand times that I do not want to collaborate with your former spouse, yet will she listen?" Diamond earrings winked as she shook her head. "She just keeps raising the offer."

"Geraldine has asked you to collaborate with Robert?"

Blue eyes widened with fake innocence. "Why yes… Oh, dear." Her lips turned down in an equally false moue. "Didn't he tell you?"

"Robert's career is no longer any business of mine." Or

wouldn't be, once the courts gave her the right to the name she'd worked so hard to establish.

"Damn. He didn't tell you." Another shake of her head. "Why, that scoundrel. He assured me that you knew Buffy and Geraldine were considering me to take over the Roberta Grace pseudonym...."

"That's a bit premature," Grace said mildly. Lucas admired the way she managed to pull herself together so quickly after having the floor pulled out from under her. "Since Robert doesn't have legal rights to the name."

"True. But I was led to believe that Penbrook Press does."

This was the first she'd heard of that. Grace hadn't known it was possible to feel hot and cold at the same time. "I think you must be mistaken," she said, with a calm that she was a very long way from feeling.

"Perhaps. Gracious, it's all such a mess, isn't it?" Anne's voice was thick with a sympathy that Grace didn't buy for a minute. "I truly believe that your would-be assassin shot at the wrong half of the Roberta Grace team, darling. Why, if I were you, after all he'd done to me—"

"But you're not."

"Not what?"

"Not me," Grace stated.

"Well, of course I'm not." This time the hand went to her throat, where more diamonds flashed. "And I do hope I didn't cause you any distress with my little news flash. Especially since I haven't made up my mind. I mean, why should I write under your name, when my own is legendary in this business?"

"That's a very good point." Grace's tone was friendly, her smile once again as false as the one being directed her way.

"On the other hand, Geraldine's offer is more than generous," Anne mused. "Which it would have to be, of course, to get me to work with that man." She turned back toward Lucas. "He must be going crazy, thinking of you *guarding* our Grace."

Her husky voice was thick with sexual innuendo. Grace found it interesting that only moments earlier Anne had implied a woman like her couldn't interest such a man, but was now suggesting they had an intimate relationship.

Anne smiled up at Lucas. "If I'm ever in need of a bodyguard, I will definitely keep you in mind, Lucas Kincaid." She skimmed a glance down him and sighed dramatically. "It would almost be worth getting shot at."

Since there was no possible safe answer to that, Lucas opted not to say anything.

"Well, as much as I've enjoyed running into you again, Grace, dear, and, of course, meeting you, Lucas, I'm afraid I must dash. I promised Kevin I'd meet with him to discuss my thoughts for my new cover. I just know he's going to make the most delicious Viking."

Grace followed her gaze across the room to where Kevin was leaning against a marble pillar, arms folded against his chest. He was wearing a black silk shirt and tight black leather pants. When she inadvertently caught his eye, he scowled at her.

"A naked Viking," Grace guessed.

"Of course. Some of us are traditionalists," Anne informed Grace haughtily. "We rather like having naked hunks on the covers of our books." That said, she turned and walked away, her hips, accentuated by the pink peplum, swaying seductively.

"And in our beds," Grace muttered as she watched the couple embrace.

"Jealous?" Lucas asked mildly.

"Not at all." Truer words had never been spoken. What woman would want a pretend hero when she had a real one standing right beside her? "Anne just gets on my nerves."

"I'd say she was aiming at your most sensitive one when she brought up your ex."

"True. That does bother me. But not because she might be sleeping with him—"

"I don't recall her saying that."

"Not even Anne's that blatant." She watched as the embrace grew increasingly intimate. If the writer were any closer, she'd be inside those leather pants. And the way Kevin's hand was cupping her silk-clad bottom, well, there wasn't any doubt as to what their meeting was really going to be about. "But she's notorious for sleeping around. And although Robert's married, that's never stopped him before."

"The Queen of Romance and the Rat." Lucas studied Grace's face as he took hold of her hand and linked their fingers together. "Sounds kinda like a fairy tale."

"Penned by the Brothers Grimm." She laughed, expelling the tension that had been writhing inside her like a ball of poisonous snakes since Anne had dropped her bombshell about one more possible adversary in the pseudonym war. "Thank you. For making me laugh when I wanted to scream."

"Any time." He lifted her hand to his lips. "But believe me, sugar, the idea of making you scream is proving damn appealing, too."

A different sort of nerves, the kind Grace was beginning to associate with Lucas, started humming from deep inside her, echoing outward, as if she'd suddenly turned into a human tuning fork.

They were standing there as if they were the only two people in the lobby, him looking down at her, Grace looking up at him, when Marianne Tyler came rushing up to them.

"Thank goodness I've found you. We're running a little late—the police insisted on searching the room for a bomb, if you can believe that—but you're on in five minutes."

The silver thread of desire that had been strung so tightly between them snapped. Grace didn't know whether to feel frustration or relief.

"A bomb?" Lucas asked sharply. "Was a threat called in?"

"Oh, no, the detective assured me they wanted to do a sweep as a preventive measure." Marianne shook her head. "I cannot believe this latest complication. The worst thing that has ever happened before at an RNN convention was that hotel fire several years ago. I'll just die if I go down as the only coordinator who suffered a murder on her watch...."

Her strained voice drifted off as she seemed to realize where that particular thought was headed. "Not that what I'm going through is anything like what you're experiencing, of course, Grace," she said quickly. "Thank goodness you're fortunate to have Mr. Kincaid to watch over you."

Grace had grown tired of lying about Lucas. Especially when it was obvious that no one was going to believe her. "Yes." She exchanged a look with him, which while brief, still made her blood sizzle. "I am lucky."

As they walked toward the ballroom where she was scheduled to give her speech, Grace could literally feel Lucas concentrating on everything and everyone around them. She knew he wasn't happy about her sticking to her schedule, but she'd insisted that her would-be assailant wouldn't dare try to strike in such a public forum. Last night had been different. People had been milling around the room, the music was loud, the mood festive. No one had been paying attention to either her or the gunman.

But this morning was an entirely different situation, she'd argued as they'd ridden down in the elevator. Conference attendees would all be seated during her speech; there was no way anyone could make another attempt on her life and escape.

"I'll be fine," she assured him yet again.

"That's the plan," he agreed gruffly, his eyes roving over the crowd streaming into the room.

After Grace was introduced in glowing terms, Lucas stood off to the side, not far from the podium. She was, he noticed, neither a practiced nor polished orator. Her nerves were more than obvious as she started out, a little rough, her hands and her voice shaky, her face pale, but tinged with a faint underlying tint of green. She'd written the speech down on neat little five-by-seven note cards, which she discarded less than three minutes into her keynote address.

"I had all these wonderful, intelligent thoughts about our business I wanted to share with you," she said. "But instead, if you don't mind, I believe I'd feel more comfortable speaking from the heart."

Nearly two thousand heads nodded in unison, as if controlled by the giant hand of a master puppeteer. There was a sprinkling of applause. Then a hush of palpable anticipation.

For the next forty-five minutes Lucas watched as Grace held her audience spellbound, sharing her own love of writing, her belief in romance, the pride and pleasure she felt writing in the popular genre that stressed relationship and family over violence and horror. She waxed eloquent when she moved on to describe the special bond between writer and reader.

Then she thanked her editors for making her books better, never suggesting she alter her personal writer's voice, and always encouraging her to take risks. She expressed appreciation for all her friends in the business who'd proven so supportive during these past difficult months, which was, everyone realized, a discreet reference to her divorce and subsequent legal problems. And then she thanked her readers, for their letters, and for buying her books, allowing her to tell her story to a wider audience. To "leave my name on the cave wall," she said.

By the time she was finished, a hush had come over the room. Then, after she'd thanked the committee again for the honor of addressing the peers she respected so, the place exploded in a hot rush of applause.

Although it was obvious that more than a few fans wanted an opportunity to speak to her, she'd promised Lucas that she wouldn't linger at the podium, where she provided such a good target, any longer than necessary.

"I'm impressed," Lucas said as they walked down the hall, back toward the lobby elevators.

"And surprised?"

"Not at all. But it's got to take a lot of guts to stand up and talk in front of a crowd like that. Even without someone gunning for you."

"Do you know, I forgot all about that while I was speaking. I guess I can only be terrified of one thing at a time."

"Makes sense to me," he said agreeably.

His hand was on her back, in a part protective, part possessive manner. Once again Grace thought how safe she felt with him. "Oh damn," she murmured.

"What?"

She sensed his increased tension. "Geraldine's headed this way. I have this feeling she's going to ask about the cruise tonight."

Lucas had been of two minds about the scheduled cruise ever since he'd learned of it. He didn't like the idea of being out in the bay, isolated from police or possible backup if anything did happen. Then again, if this letter writer was a crazy fan or writer, at least Grace would be safe among her peers. Or reasonably safe, he considered, thinking about her former husband and the barracuda Queen of Romance.

"That was a marvelous speech, Grace!" The publisher touched cheeks, greeting Grace with an enthusiasm that gave the impression they were long-lost friends, instead of two business acquaintances who'd been together in Grace's suite only this morning. "George and I were so proud of you, weren't we, Georgie?" she asked the editorial director.

"Of course we were," he answered distractedly, as he shifted the Lhasa apso, which was squirming in his arms like the nightcrawlers Grace used to bait a hook with when she'd go fishing with her father.

"I only wish you could have seen fit to name the company," Geraldine added. "Or at the very least the title of your upcoming book."

"I thanked my editors by name. But the speech was about the appeal of our genre," Grace answered quietly. "It wasn't meant to be a publicity device."

"Darling, if you're going to take over Robert's job promoting the Roberta Grace name, you are going to have to understand that *all* appearances are about publicity. Or there's just no point in wasting your time."

"But I didn't find it a waste of time."

"Then it's obvious you need to learn to prioritize," the publisher snapped back. Then she exhaled. "Oh dear, let's not get into this now. I just wanted to make certain that you'd be on the Penbrook cruise tonight."

Penbrook Press's annual author bash was always the hottest ticket at the conference. This year's formal dinner cruise, complete with a Fourth of July fireworks display over the bay, promised to live up to previous events.

"I'm not certain—"

"Oh, you must. I'd planned for you to sit at our table."

"With Robert?"

"No. It's one thing to want the two of you to provide a united front for the awards banquet. However, this dinner isn't staged for public consumption. We're family, after all."

As Geraldine patted her arm in an almost maternal manner, Grace knew she was sunk. "I'll be there."

"That's my girl." The publisher's smile suggested she'd never expected any other outcome. "Well, I must run. I promised Anne Kilgallen we'd do brunch."

"Speaking of Anne," Grace said, "she tells me you've asked her to work with Robert."

"Oh, it wasn't an actual offer," Geraldine said quickly. Too quickly, Grace thought. "We were merely discussing possibilities. In the event that Robert does end up with the Roberta Grace name."

"He won't." Grace lifted her chin. "So that's one possibility you needn't concern yourself with." That stated, she turned toward Lucas. "Didn't you say something about my checking out of my room?"

"You're leaving the hotel?"

"I thought it would be easier to guard Grace if she wasn't staying in the conference hotel," Lucas explained. "As it is, she already has more public appearances than I'd like."

"Well, I suppose that makes sense." Geraldine's brow furrowed as she considered the implications of this unforeseen event. "What hotel will you be moving to?"

"I'm afraid I'm not at liberty to say."

"What?" The furrows deepened.

"It's nothing personal," Lucas assured her. "But in order for me to do my job right, I have to be allowed to handle things my way. Which means keeping some information on a need-to-know basis."

"And you don't think Grace's publisher is one of those who needs to know?"

"No, ma'am, I don't." When the older woman looked as if she were on the verge of an explosion, he flashed her a slow smile that, despite the serious topic being discussed, Grace found distractingly sexy. "Think of it as insurance," he suggested. "If the bad guys take you hostage in an attempt to get to Gracie, you won't have to worry about spilling the beans when they torture you."

Geraldine paled at that, but only fleetingly. Then her gaze turned speculative. "You are a very strange man, Mr. Kincaid."

"So people have told me, Ms. Manning. But I also know my business. As you know yours."

The implication was crystal clear: since he wasn't about to tell Geraldine Manning how to publish books, she shouldn't try to tell him how to protect Grace.

"Well, that's reassuring. After all, we all want to keep Grace safe so she can keep writing those wonderful bestselling novels for Penbrook." She flashed another smile Grace's way. "As I said, darling, you're a tremendously important asset to our little publishing family." That said, she swept off, George trailing behind her, still struggling with Dalai, who snarled at a passing agent.

"You're a tremendously important asset to our little publishing family, darling," Grace muttered, impressing Lucas with her impersonation skills as she hit the publisher's tony British accent right on.

"The Addams Family, perhaps," he drawled. "Quite a snake pit you're working in, darlin'. It's coming as a revelation that there are so many vipers lurking behind the hearts-and-flowers facade."

"Even the Garden of Eden had its serpent," Grace

noted. "And actually, considering the high stakes involved in publishing, most everyone in the romance field is amazingly supportive of one another.

"The business might get a little bit crazy, and there are times I feel as if I'm on a roller coaster, but it's still the best E-ticket ride going. I love it." Her gaze drifted across the lobby to where Geraldine and the self-proclaimed Queen of Romance were disappearing into the Windjammer Restaurant for their brunch. "Most of the time, anyway."

Grace sighed and decided she could only tackle one problem at a time. There wasn't any point in worrying about Anne writing under her name unless she lost her court case. Which, she vowed yet again, she had no intention of allowing to happen.

Thirty minutes later, she'd finished packing and was waiting for the valet to bring Lucas's car around from the hotel parking garage.

"Nice," she murmured as the black Porsche pulled up in front of the bronze revolving door. "The bodyguard business must pay very well."

"I do okay. Actually, the car was an indulgence from a business deal that turned out well." He opened the passenger door for her.

Grace settled into the glove-soft bucket seat and inhaled the leathery new-car smell. "You haven't had it long," she said when he joined her in the cockpitlike interior.

"Bought it six months ago." He ran his palm over the walnut steering wheel. "It's one of the few things I'm going to miss."

"That's quite an indulgence," she murmured. "Spending all that money for just six months."

"True." He put the car in gear and pulled out of the circular driveway. "I've always wanted one, but never stayed anywhere long enough to make it worthwhile. Besides," he added, "one of the other guys in the office is buying it from me when I leave, so it's not entirely a loss."

Grace was curious what sort of business deal Lucas had been involved in, but since the day had dawned surprisingly bright and sunny for a city with a reputation for cloudy skies, she decided just to enjoy the drive in this sleek black sports car.

It was one of those days that made Lucas understand how Tony Bennett could have left his heart in San Francisco. Sunbathers had taken up nearly every inch of the bottle green grass of Union Square, soaking up the rays while eating their lunch beneath the benevolent blue sky. A breeze from the bay kept temperatures cool enough to be comfortable.

It truly was a lovely city, he thought as he drove past a towheaded toddler tossing pieces torn off a hot dog bun to a clutch of speckled gray-and-white pigeons. If Lucas were the type of man to settle down, he could certainly think of worse places to put down roots. Which he'd have to do sometime.

Having followed his jet-fighter-pilot father from navy base to navy base, Lucas couldn't count the number of schools he'd attended. He could remember the day he'd decided never to inflict the same fate on his kids. He'd been a junior in high school when he'd been forced to leave his championship baseball team right before the state all-star game, where he'd been voted first baseman.

The four years he'd spent at the academy at Annapolis had been the longest he'd lived anywhere. Having selected the Special Warfare billet, he'd been dispatched to the navy's Basic Underwater Demolition/SEAL school in Coronado, California. From there he'd been shipped out to hot spots all over the world.

After his near fatal misadventure, Lucas had convinced himself that it only made sense to settle down. Unfortunately, after eighteen months working for S. J. Slade, he'd felt as if he'd begun to grow barnacles. There was still too much of the world he needed to see, too many inlets and too much blue water left to explore. He'd tried, unsuccessfully, to explain that to his employer. And to Fancy, who was impatient to become a great-grandmother.

"Where are we going?"

Grace's voice shattered his rare introspection. Lucas glanced into the rearview mirror again, determining that they weren't being followed. "Sausalito. I figured we'd stash you on my boat."

"Your boat?"

"The one I'm sailing to Alaska on," he reminded her. "And don't worry, it's a sixty-foot ketch, so you'll have your own quarters. And I promise to be on my best behavior."

"In the movies, the detectives always sleep with their clients."

The minute she heard the words escape her mouth, Grace couldn't believe she'd actually said them. She was going to have to be more discreet, she warned herself. Although Lucas was the sexiest man she'd ever met, she was not interested in a brief affair. And with him headed off to Alaska right after the conference, it was obvious that's all he was interested in.

"That's in the movies," he said. "And for the record, technically, I'm not a detective. I'm a bodyguard. And if you think I'm taking you away from prying eyes to sleep with you, darlin', you're wrong about my motives."

"Oh? Are you saying you don't want to sleep with me?"

"Of course I do." This time it was an *aha!* look that flashed in her remarkable eyes. "A man would have to be cold stone dead for a week of Sundays not to want to tangle the sheets with you, Gracie. But that's not the reason I took this job."

"It isn't?"

"Hell, no." He flashed her a grin. "I took the job because I thought, since I have every intention of marrying you, it might be a good idea to keep you alive to walk down the aisle." Knowing how traditional women could be when it came to weddings, Lucas decided to save the idea of getting married on the *Rebel's Reward* for later.

She stared. "Ms. Spade really should have mentioned you were crazy."

Unoffended, he shrugged. "Not crazy. Just traditional."

"You consider it traditional to propose within two days of meeting a woman?"

"Not just any woman. The Right Woman. It's a family tradition. My father proposed to my mother the day his plane crashed on the beach right outside her family's vacation home." He smiled as he thought about the story that had been woven into the fabric of family legend. "He always said that he fell for her. Right out of the sky."

"Isn't that clever," Grace said dryly.

She was, Lucas allowed, a tougher nut to crack than she'd appeared at first glance. Reminding himself that he'd always been a man to enjoy a challenge, he plowed forward. "Apparently my mama thought so. They were married three days later. They celebrated their thirty-fifth anniversary this June."

"That's nice," she said.

"We think so." Lucas considered thirty-five years with this woman a good start. "My grandpappy Virgil was a bit slower. It took him a week to talk my grandma Fancy into running off with him against her daddy's wishes. She came from a rich planter's family who didn't think a man who sailed the seven seas was good enough for their only daughter, the belle of Raintree County.

"After they eloped, she was cut off from her family. Her name was even crossed off the family Bible. I've seen it," he added, in case Grace might think him guilty of embellishing.

As he'd hoped, the story of forbidden love was too rich for her romance writer's heart to ignore. "Did her parents ever relent?"

"Oh, sure. When my daddy was born nine months to the day after their wedding. They might have been stubborn, and they might not have approved of Fancy's choice, but they were too tickled about bein' grandparents to keep a decent pique going."

She smiled at that. "That's nice."

"We've always thought so." He switched lanes, then glanced in the rearview mirror again. "We Kincaid men always know the right woman when we see her," he explained. "It's a knack. Fancy says it's a kind of second sight we brought with us from Scotland. Along with our determination. And, of course, our devastating good looks."

"Not to mention your humility." Her tone was cool, but amused.

"That, too," he agreed good-naturedly. "The thing is, I'm a patient man, Gracie. I'm willin' to wait until you realize I'm right about us being a perfect match."

She shook her head again, but her lips quirked in a way that suggested she was fighting back a reluctant smile. "You're definitely not like any other man I've ever met."

"You hit that nail on the head. But, of course, I could tell you were a clever woman the minute I walked into the oyster bar." Actually, her mind hadn't been the first thing that had attracted him to her, but Lucas saw no reason to complicate matters by quibbling over unimportant details. He reached out, captured her hand and held it between them. "Now that you've figured out that I'm one of a kind, falling in love with me is going to be as easy as falling off a log."

She tugged her hand loose. "Into a pit of alligators."

Not a man to be easily deterred, or offended, he laughed.

"I've already been married," she commented.

"Hey, I'm not going to hold that little mistake against you." He shrugged. "At my age, I can't expect a virgin bride anyway. If I wanted one. Which I don't."

"Well, that certainly comes as a relief." They were approaching the soaring orange span of the Golden Gate Bridge. "So, how much sexual experience should your ideal female have?"

"Since my daddy taught me that a gentleman never kisses and tells, it follows that I don't have any business asking a woman about her past dalliances. What you did before you met me doesn't count, Grace. Because we're both starting fresh right here and now."

"There's something you need to understand. This is a difficult time for me...."

"I can understand that," he said helpfully. "After all, it's got to be upsetting, worrying about some crackpot taking potshots at you. But believe me, Gracie, I'm not going to let that happen."

"That wasn't what I was talking about.... Well, that, too," she admitted, in what seemed to be an afterthought. "But what with the divorce, and losing my editor, the court battle over my name, not to mention beginning contract negotiations, I have neither the time nor the inclination for an affair."

"Okay." He surprised her by agreeing easily. "How about a three-night stand?"

"What happened to marriage?"

"Oh, that's still on the drawing board. But since you have so many distractions right now, I figured the idea might be less threatening if you thought of it as merely sex."

For not the first time since meeting this man, Grace found herself smiling at his easygoing attitude. "You really are impossible."

"And right," he said, taking her hand again and lifting it to his lips. Heat shot from her fingertips all the way to her toes.

"I don't believe in love." And hadn't for a very long time.

"Liar," he countered without heat as he laced their fingers together and rested their joined hands on his thigh. "It's obvious from your writing that you're a card-carrying romantic, sugar."

"You read one of my books?" Pleasure mixed with anxiety born from a disconcerting need to know what he thought caused a tremor in her stomach.

"Last night. I had a bellman go buy one at the hotel gift shop. The one about the outlaw."

"*Desperado.*"

"Yeah. I liked it. A lot, actually. It was an exciting story and you hooked me from the first line."

She could feel herself beaming. There was no other word for it. And although once again Grace told herself that a compliment from this man should not mean so much, it did.

"You're a romantic, Gracie," Lucas repeated, nodding to himself. "And since meeting you, I've realized that I am, too." Which had come as a surprise. "That's why we're destined for one of your happily-ever-after endings."

The idea, as fantastic as it was, proved frighteningly appealing. As they crossed over the bay, Grace sternly reminded herself that a sensible woman, a woman who'd already been burned once by her emotions, could not possibly fall in love in two short days.

Beside her, Lucas looked out at the sun-spangled blue ocean and imagined making love to his new bride beneath an Alaskan midnight sun.

8

SAUSALITO, located just across the Golden Gate Bridge, was a charming little Mediterranean-type village nestled along the shoreline, reminding Grace of the French Riviera. Rustic houses, quaint Victorians and soaring homes of redwood and glass crowded the hillsides, cascading down steep slopes to the sparkling blue bay. Grace was immediately charmed.

"Oh, it's lovely," she said as Lucas drove past the restaurants and shops lining Bridgeway Avenue. A sign at the marina declared the town to be a Nuclear Free Zone. In a bit of whimsy, another beside it announced it was also a Cholesterol Free Zone.

"It's definitely more laid-back than the city." He pulled the Porsche into the parking lot of the yacht club.

"Which is why it appeals to you," she guessed.

He shrugged. "I suppose cities have their appeal. And San Francisco is definitely one of the most appealing. If you like the fast life."

"Which you don't?" A man who enjoyed life in the urban fast lane probably wouldn't be heading off to watch whales in Alaska.

Although her tone was casual, Lucas had the feeling that her reason for asking was more serious. Which is why he decided to answer honestly. "I'd rather be sailing."

Her smile was quick and warm and pleased. "Me, too."

That hurdle behind him, Lucas took their bags out of

the car and began walking down the dock. The breeze blowing off the bay carried the scent of the sea, of salt and seaweed and exotic, faraway places.

In the distance, across the water, San Francisco gleamed golden in the sunshine like a grand dame wearing her best jewels. Moorings creaked as the boats bobbed on the water. Gulls whirled overhead, searching out fish or a tourist who'd prove generous with his french fries.

It was a perfect day. Almost too nice for thoughts of murder. It occurred to Lucas that he'd spent his entire adult life thinking about death. How to avoid his own, how to dispatch an enemy and then, during those days in that rat-infested Caribbean prison, how to stay out of the clutches of the grim reaper one day at a time.

Even the past eighteen months had focused on keeping clients from getting murdered. Even more reason, Lucas considered, why, after this conference was over, the closest he wanted to come to death would be a James Patterson thriller.

The *Rebel's Reward* was berthed at the end of the dock. As he approached, Lucas felt that now familiar surge of pleasure at the sight of her sleek white hull.

He'd come a long way since the twenty-four-foot sloop he'd picked up at a bargain-basement price from a former SEAL living in Hawaii, whose wife had decided that the growing family needed a minivan more than a sailboat. The boats may have gotten bigger and more expensive, but Lucas's love of life on the water hadn't changed.

"Oh!" Grace drew in an appreciative breath as Lucas stopped in front of the ketch. "She's absolutely gorgeous!"

Her honest, open appreciation assured him that he'd chosen exactly the right woman to fall in love with. "I like her," he said mildly, not fooling either of them with his false modesty.

As he helped her onto the gleaming teak deck, Grace tried to match this boat, which must have cost a fortune, with the laid-back bodyguard whale watcher, and failed.

"What did you do?" she asked, running a hand over the gleaming brass rail, "discover a lost treasure ship? Or win her in a high-stakes poker game?" Now that she could imagine.

"It was a game, all right. But the computer kind. Virtual reality, actually. I invented one."

"You invented a computer game?" She was discovering facets she never would have imagined. But then again, she'd only met him yesterday. "Like kids play in an arcade?"

He shrugged. "It didn't start out that way. I originally developed the program for the Pentagon."

"I see." She shook her head and stared at him. "No, actually, I don't. In fact, I'm having difficulty understanding what a man who could develop computer software for the Pentagon would be doing playing bodyguard to a romance writer."

"Not just any romance writer," he reminded her. "I told you, the minute I saw you—"

"I know. You fell in love." As flattering as it was, as often as she'd written about love at first sight, Grace still wasn't sure she believed in such a thing.

He rubbed his jaw and gave her a slow, measuring look. "Well, to be perfectly honest, it was probably more lust at first sight. But by the time I was lying on top of you in the Golden Gate Ballroom, I was definitely smitten."

She couldn't help smiling at that. "So, why did you become a bodyguard in the first place?"

Another shrug. "Eighteen months ago I was out of work when I got a phone call from Samantha Slade. She was looking to expand her bodyguard agency and a friend had recommended me. Since I'd just gone off the wagon and was looking for a new direction in my life, I accepted her offer. Our deal allowed me to take only as many clients as I wanted, which left time to work on my program."

"The Pentagon software."

"Yeah."

"Can you talk about it? What does it do?"

"It's kind of complicated to explain, but I suppose you can say it's an antiterrorist game. The government paid handsomely enough for it, but then, by one of those funny quirks of fate, it fell into the hands of an admiral whose daughter just happens to be the head of a gaming software company based in Menlo Park. She asked me to come up with a consumer version, and, as they say, the rest is history." He glanced around the ketch with unmistakable pride.

"So now you're rich."

"Filthy. Is that a problem?"

"Are you kidding?" She laughed. "I've already been married to one man who only wanted my money...." Her voice drifted off as she realized what she'd been about to say. "Not that I thought you were anything like Robert."

"I appreciate that greatly, darlin'." His lips quirked as he tugged on a tawny strand of hair that had escaped today's tidy knot.

"And I'm not in the market for marriage."

"That's all right," he agreed easily. "You've had a lot on your mind the past couple days, so I won't push. For now, at least. Then, after the conference wraps up, I'll have all the way to Alaska to change your mind."

"What makes you think I'll even sail to Alaska with you?"

It was not an outright refusal. Lucas figured he was definitely making headway. "Because you can't resist my Southern charm?" His fingers trailed down her cheek.

"Because you tremble when I touch you?" Around her lips, which parted instinctively at the butterfly-light touch. "Because you want me as much as I want you?"

He lowered his head and touched his mouth to hers in a brief whisper of a kiss. "Because you can't resist the idea of taking this sleek lady out onto the high seas and racing wherever the wind blows?"

Her lips softened beneath his; her bones felt as if they were melting in the summer sun. "Is this a multiple choice test?"

"In a way." His lips plucked at hers. Teasing, tasting, tantalizing. He'd somehow managed to rid himself of the cases he'd been carrying beneath his arm and gathered her closer, so she could feel his warmth. "Pick an answer, Gracie." His hands were kneading her waist. "Any answer."

If she were to be totally honest, she'd have to choose them all. "I'll think about it," she whispered instead against his mouth.

He lifted his head and smiled down at her. "That's my girl." Then his head swooped down again, like a seabird crashing into the surf.

Desire rose, a soaring tide in a storm-tossed sea. Her mind fogged as she clung to him while the ketch bobbed gently on the water. The mooring ropes made a low moaning sound as they rubbed against the dock. Rigging creaked, the wheeling gulls continued to cry, but with her blood roaring like the crash of waves in her ears, Grace could hear none of those familiar, beloved sea sounds.

Her response was as it had been before—hot and fast. And gloriously sweet. Lucas had already grown accustomed to wanting her; he figured he'd still feel this grinding, delicious need when they were in their nineties. But because the need was threatening to swamp the desire, because he was tempted to drag her down onto the deck he'd spent days sanding and polishing, he managed, just barely, to once again back away from the edge.

He'd spent nearly his entire adult life on boats, but never had he felt as if the deck was tilting so dangerously beneath his feet. The only other time he'd felt like this was when he'd been deep-sea diving off the coast of New Zealand and had surfaced too fast from fathoms below. "One request." He skimmed a not-very-steady finger down her nose. "Think fast."

Emotions and words tangled in Grace's throat, preventing speech. All she could do was nod.

To her relief, the sexual tension eased for the time being as Lucas gave her a tour of the sixty-foot ketch. She did not have to pretend to be impressed as she oohed and aahed over the three staterooms; two heads, one with a tub and shower, the other with a shower; a spacious salon with an entertainment center; and galley complete with refrigerator-freezer, propane stove with eye-level oven, and microwave. There was even a washer and dryer and, amazingly, a diesel fireplace in the main stateroom.

"It's nice on cold, rainy nights," Lucas explained when she expressed surprise.

"I can imagine." Too well, she discovered, as she pictured herself lying in that wide king-size berth with Lucas, while the rain pelted the overhead deck and a warm fire blazed. "She truly is a marvelous boat, Lucas."

She dragged her gaze from that all-too-enticing bed and looked around the room. The wide windows allowed the daylight in, avoiding any submarine feeling; sunshine made the hand-rubbed cherry interior gleam like glass.

"My father always wanted a ketch like this," she said. "He used to talk about it a lot. We had a twenty-five foot sloop we'd take out on the Chesapeake, and I'd fantasize about the day I became a bestselling author and would be able to buy him his dream boat."

"You knew that young that you wanted to write?"

"I think I was born a writer. My mother thought I should study something safe, to have a job to fall back on, like teaching, or something in the medical or computer professions. But I was always afraid I'd get stuck in a rut. Or worse yet, become comfortable there."

"I've always thought safe was a close cousin to boring," Lucas agreed. Even the debacle in the Caribbean hadn't changed his mind about that.

Because her scent, which had blossomed in the close quarters, was already beginning to drive him crazy, and the nearby bed was proving too tempting, Lucas decided the time had come to put some distance between them. He touched his knuckles to her cheek. "I'll let you unpack."

How did he do it? Grace wondered yet again. How was it possible that all he had to do was to touch her, or even look at her in that warm, bone-melting way, to cause her mind to go as clear as glass? Because she wanted to cover his hand with hers, because she wanted to grab hold of him and pull him down onto that inviting bed, she backed away ever so slightly.

"Thank you."

"And then you can come out and work on the deck in the sun."

"I'd like that."

"And then I'll fix us lunch."

"You don't have to go to that much trouble."

"It's no trouble. Besides, I stocked the larder for the trip, so I might as well use up some of the food."

The trip to Alaska. The trip he would have already been on if she'd called that 1-800 number a mere hour later. Having become accustomed to charting her own course, and having been burned by the mistaken youthful idea of Robert as her soul mate, Grace no longer believed in destiny. Still, as she went to work, unpacking her suitcases for the second time in two days, she was forced to wonder.

Since he'd rattled her from the beginning, Grace was surprised at how relaxed she felt with Lucas. She was also grateful she'd planned to spend a few days in wine country after the conference and had packed some casual clothes that were perfect for wearing on the boat.

They were both out on the deck, each working away on their laptop computers, aware of the other, but not so much that they couldn't concentrate on their individual work. Grace was working on her new book, the one coincidentally with a pirate hero.

A few feet away, trying to ignore how good she smelled and how darn cute and intense she looked in those oversize glasses, Lucas was on-line, skimming through Penbrook Press's accounting system. There were times, and this was definitely one of them, that he was grateful for the covert computer skills the navy had taught him.

From what he could tell, the publishing company had gone into the red to pay high advances on a series of celebrity biographies, several written by participants in the type of crime stories that were usually consigned to the covers of tabloid newspapers. Since their previous publishing lists hadn't included any such books, Lucas could only conclude that Geraldine Manning was the force behind the editorial change.

A few more keystrokes took him into the publisher's mainframe mailboxes, where he located internal memos from Manning to the top management at the parent company, Dwyer's Drier Diapers, confirming Lucas's guess. Since Dwyer had gone public, they were no longer a family business, but were answerable to stockholders.

Which was why she'd been appointed publisher. After a stunning success selling the disposable diapers to the lucrative Asian markets, she'd recklessly promised the board of directors a twenty-five percent profit on their investment within the first eighteen months. Although Lucas wasn't that familiar with the logistics of the publishing business, he suspected that she was going to have to pull some very clever rabbits out of her hat to live up to her pledge.

Which, of course, should have taken her off his list of suspects, since a check of the Rainbow Romances' profit-and-loss statement revealed that Grace was the company's most profitable author. Geraldine might be a pain in the ass, and she might be a gambler, but he couldn't think of any reason a publisher would want to kill the goose who laid the golden books.

He was about to explore further when the system suddenly shut down, disconnecting his modem.

When three additional attempts wouldn't even let him into the system, he gave up and went back into the cabin.

Because he'd promised Grace lunch, and because he always thought better on a full stomach, Lucas went to work peeling the shrimp he planned to grill.

"This is heaven."

As she sat down at the table Lucas had set up on the deck, Grace tried to remember when she'd ever felt more relaxed and came up blank.

"If you think this is nice, wait until we get to Alaska."

"I haven't said I was going yet," she reminded him as she put her napkin on her lap.

"You haven't said you won't, either." He opened the green bottle of Pouilly-Fumé, poured a stemmed glass and set it in front of her, where the white wine shimmered like liquid gold in the afternoon sunshine. Lucas popped the cap on a bottle of non-alcoholic beer for himself.

"True." She took a sip of the smooth wine. "But that's just because it's too lovely a day to argue." She leaned

back in the chair and watched as he took the shrimp ka-
bobs off the barbecue. "If I'd known that catering was
part of a bodyguard's duties, I think I would have hired
one years ago."

He laughed at that as he slid the shrimp and grilled
vegetables onto the plate atop rice pilaf. "I like good food,
but I'm not much for getting dressed up and going out, so
I finally figured out that if I didn't want to keep settling
for cold cuts and Chinese take-out, it might be a good idea
to teach myself the way around a galley."

The shrimp was gingered. And delicious. "For a self-
taught man, you've definitely risen to the head of the
class."

"Thank you, darlin'." His grin was quick and easy.
When it made her want to throw herself at him, Grace resisted the impulse and took another bite of shrimp instead. "Come sail the seven seas with me, and I'll cook
you lunch every day, dinner every night, and serve you
breakfast in bed every morning."

"I don't eat breakfast."

"Ah, but you'll need to. To keep your strength up."
When he waggled his brows in a rakish way, Grace
couldn't help but laugh.

Despite the threat on her life that had been the reason
for them meeting in the first place, the mood remained
light. Over a lunch of shrimp, rice, salad and crunchy
sourdough rolls that could rival any five-star restaurant
in the city, Grace found herself telling Lucas all about her
family, while he shared stories about his own admiral father, who'd recently retired from the Pentagon to spend
his days playing golf, and his mother, an antique dealer
who'd recently had her first professional showing of wa-
tercolor paintings.

"I think that's lovely, that she could start a new career

at this stage of her life," Grace said. "What does your father think of it?"

"He's pleased as punch. Although I did hear they had a few tense days when he first retired and decided that he'd rearrange her studio to make it more efficient. But he dropped that idea when Mom threatened him with a divorce, then bought him a new set of Ping golf clubs and sent him out to get some daily exercise."

Grace laughed again. "So, how do you think he'd feel if she became rich and famous?"

"Terrific. Why wouldn't he?"

"Well, although he was obviously successful in his own work, some men might have trouble sharing the spotlight."

"We Kincaid men have never needed spotlights shining on us to remind us who—and what—we are." He reached across the table to toy with the ring on her finger. "And if this is a roundabout way of asking me if I'd have any problems with being married to the rich and famous Roberta Grace, you don't have to worry your gorgeous head about that."

"I shouldn't think so. Since you're obviously richer than I am."

"I just might be." He knew he was because he'd just read her royalty statement. But not richer by much. "But I'd feel the same if I were just an unemployed bodyguard. In fact," he mused, rubbing his jaw with his free hand, "now that I think about it, the idea of bein' your boy toy definitely has its appeal, sugar."

He wasn't the only one who found the idea appealing. "I'll keep that in mind," Grace murmured.

And keep it in mind she did during the rest of the afternoon, while her fictional hero kept taking on more and more of Lucas's attributes. Thoughts of Lucas occupied her during her shower, and while dressing for the Penbrook Press cruise, which she'd just as soon skip, but didn't dare. Especially now that she knew Robert was angling to have Geraldine decide the Roberta Grace name belonged to the publisher, who might then hand it over to him.

As Grace leaned close to the mirror to put on her lipstick, Lucas's statement about being her boy toy flashed through her mind yet again. Although she knew he'd been joking, she also knew that Robert wouldn't be above sleeping with Geraldine, if that's what it took to clinch the deal. The only problem, she thought wickedly, was that in his case it would undoubtedly blow his chances of ever publishing with Penbrook again.

Wishing the boat had a full-length mirror, she backed up as far as possible, and decided that what she could see looked pretty darn good. The dress was far more romantic than she was accustomed to wearing, but when she'd first seen it in the window at Saks, she'd fallen in love with it. It had reminded her of the type of gown Cinderella might wear to the ball.

She left the stateroom and entered the salon, where Lucas was waiting. From the way his eyes darkened as they swept over her, she decided that perhaps she'd just garnered a personal best.

"Thank you." His voice was husky, echoing the hunger in his eyes.

"For what?"

"For wearing that dress." He allowed another longer look. Above the beaded, strapless top that showed off her spectacular cleavage, her shoulders were bare, inviting a man's touch. His lips. The long skirt was a swirl of chiffon and white lace that hinted at the wraparound legs beneath. "If I hadn't already fallen in love with you, this would definitely clinch it."

"Don't tell me you're so shallow as to judge a woman by her looks."

"Of course not." He picked up a flute of champagne he'd just poured, crossed the room and handed it to her. "I'm a sucker for brains and wit and spunk, all of which you have in spades. But the fact that you look as tasty as the whipped cream on top of a hot fudge sundae is definitely the icing on the cake, to strain a metaphor."

Although she considered herself reasonably attractive, Grace had never really thought of herself as a beautiful woman. Until yesterday, when she'd begun looking at herself through Lucas's eyes. And while deep down inside she believed that he was prejudiced, Grace decided to enjoy the illusion.

"Speaking of looking good…" It was her turn to skim a glance over him. "You're certainly very handsome tonight."

That was the understatement of the century. As she took a sip of the champagne, Grace decided that taking Lucas to the dinner cruise would be like tossing him into a tank of man-eating barracudas. "Although I suppose it must come in handy in the bodyguard business, I wouldn't have guessed that you'd have much use for a custom-tailored tux in Alaska."

"That's what I was thinking when I was about to put it in the bag with the stuff for the Salvation Army. Then, at the last minute, for some reason I decided to hang on to it for a while longer. Just goes to show you can't duck your destiny."

"I've never believed in destiny."

"Neither have I. Until you."

When she felt herself drowning in his dark eyes again, Grace wondered what would happen if they just let the cruise boat sail without them.

"Lucas…"

"I know. You want to take things slow."

"No." She ran her fingernail around the rim of the flute as she met his now frustrated gaze with a reasonably level one of her own. "What I want is for you to drag me into your stateroom, rip this outrageously expensive dress off my body and spend the rest of the night ravishing me. And letting me do the same to you."

"Now there's a plan."

"But I'm not an impulsive woman. I make lists of things I'm going to do every day. Then I color code the lists. My outlines for my books have been known to run nearly a hundred pages. I never buy anything without first checking with *Consumer Reports* and—"

"And you never sleep with a man you've just met."

"Exactly." She was relieved he understood.

"Let me ask you something."

"What?"

"How long did you know the Rat before you slept with him?"

"Six months."

"And how long after that did you get married?"

"Eighteen months."

"So, we're talking about a total of two years, right?"

Grace saw where he was going and tried to head him off. "That's right, but—"

"There's no buts about it, Gracie. You spent two years with the Rat and you were trying so darn hard to make it work, you refused to accept what was right in front of your eyes. That the guy will never be anything but a self-indulgent loser.

"Do you have any idea how much I wish I'd known you for these past two years? Hell, I wish we'd been teenage sweethearts, because I would have loved spending hot, lazy summer nights necking with you at the Raintree

Drive-in Theater and slow dancing beneath the crepe paper streamers at the senior prom."

"That sounds nice," she admitted. Grace hadn't been asked to her senior prom. Nor had she ever necked at a drive-in, although Steven Blake *had* once French kissed her in the back row of the theater during *Star Trek IV, The Voyage Home.*

"Yeah. Real nice. Better than nice, it sounds terrific.... But the thing is, Gracie, just because we missed out on all that is even more reason not to waste time now."

He skimmed a hand along her bare shoulder, pleased by her slight shiver. "Sometimes all the stars and planets are in the right place, the gods are generous and two people meet and click right off the bat. Like us." He smiled down at her, with his mouth and his eyes. "And everyone knows that the gods do not take kindly to people who reject their gifts."

"With a line like that, I'm surprised you've never considered writing a book."

"Oh, I have."

"Oh?"

She told herself she shouldn't be surprised. After all, everyone she knew—from her hairdresser, to her grocer, to the boy who delivered the pizza during her all-night writing marathons, to the limo driver who'd picked her up at the airport yesterday—all planned to someday write the Great American Novel.

And although she knew Lucas would never use her like Robert had, she would have preferred to discover he was the one individual in the world who wasn't interested in becoming a rich and famous author.

"Yeah." He watched the range of emotions move across her expressive face and decided that although Tina Parker might not be his favorite type of female, the agent was a good match for Grace. Because left on her own, the way her gorgeous face revealed her every thought, the romance writer would undoubtedly prove a lousy negotiator.

"I'm figuring it'll be a small print run. One copy, just for us. And I'm going to title it *Fifty Ways to Love Gracie*."

Because she looked like an angel and smelled like heaven, but most of all because it had been too long since he'd kissed her, he lowered his mouth to a breath away from hers. Then waited.

They stood there, his thighs pressing against the lacy white skirt, his palms smoothing her shoulders, his thumbs brushing the crest of her breasts. Lucas looking down at her, Grace looking back up at him....

She moved first, lifting a hand to his neck, her lips to his. Her mouth was hot and hungry as she kissed him in a way that was part promise, part challenge. When her teeth nipped at his bottom lip, lust razored through him. His head swam, his legs felt as if they'd gone numb from the knees down, both physical effects undoubtedly caused by all the blood rushing to more vital places.

"Only fifty ways?" she asked with a shaky laugh as the hard, impatient kiss ended.

"That's just for starters. I plan a sequel." He took hold of her waist and went back for seconds, but she was quicker, moving out of his grasp and out of range.

"I'll take your proposal under editorial consideration." Her voice was part honey, part smoke and all siren. "After the cruise."

It wasn't his first choice, which was to skip the cruise and spend the night driving each other crazy. But, Lucas reminded himself, some people considered anticipation to be part of the enjoyment. Of course, some people had never kissed Grace Fairfield.

"After the cruise," he agreed. Because all that pale flesh was too tempting, he picked up the stole she'd dropped onto the floor and wrapped it around her fragrant shoulders.

As they left the boat and walked along the dock to the parking lot where he'd left the Porsche, Lucas was whistling. Grace smiled when she recognized the tune as "Amazing Grace."

9

THE GLEAMING WHITE *Belle of the Bay* was berthed at the end of a dock at Fisherman's Wharf. Although it was still daylight, the parking lot was beginning to fill with women dressed to the nines in beaded satins and silks, full nighttime makeup and a pirate's ransom in jewels.

"I feel as if I've just stumbled into a harem," Lucas murmured as they walked across the asphalt lot to the three-story-tall ship.

"You're obviously not the only one who feels that way," Grace said as she watched the covetous glances directed their way. Although her gown had cost a small fortune, she suspected it was not the subject of such open envy.

"Grace! Lucas!"

They paused at the familiar voice. Geraldine was pushing her way through the crowd. Struggling behind her was George, carrying, as usual, Dalai. The dog was clad for the formal occasion in a billowy cloud of peach chiffon and a rhinestone collar. The publisher had opted for a more classic look, choosing a stunning white silk tuxedo that set off her silver hair. She looked rich, sleek and extremely powerful, which she was.

"Evenin', Ms. Manning," Lucas greeted her. "Don't you look as pretty as a Georgia peach tonight?"

To Grace's amazement, Geraldine actually blushed at the compliment. "Why, thank you, Mr. Kincaid. And you look incredibly dashing yourself in black tie. I don't suppose you've reconsidered freelancing as a cover model?"

"No, ma'am, I haven't."

"But you'd be so wonderful. With those chiseled cheekbones and your weathered, lived-in face, and that hair, not to mention your body, of course," she murmured as she leaned back and took a long judicious tour of the body in question, as if Lucas were a prime rib roast she was considering serving up for tonight's buffet dinner. "You'd probably do wonders for our bottom line."

"I appreciate the compliment, ma'am. But I think I'll pass."

She shook her head. "What a waste." Finally, she turned to Grace. "You look absolutely stunning, dear. I loved that dress the first time I saw it."

"It's new."

"Oh, I didn't mean on you. I ran into Buffy and your ex leaving the hotel, and she just happens to be wearing the same gown. Isn't that an amazing coincidence?"

Grace tried to tell herself it didn't matter. But it did. If any other woman were to show up wearing the same dress, she would have shrugged it off. But Buffy wasn't just any other woman, and since publishing was a very small, incestuous world, and everyone was aware of the sordid story, she knew she'd just been catapulted into the center of attention for the evening.

"It certainly is." She was proud of herself when she managed to keep her voice mild. And vaguely disinterested.

"Obviously, you and Buffy have more in common than just books and men," Geraldine decided. Her brocade bag began to ring. "Oh, damn." She paused, took out a cellular phone and flipped it open. "Geraldine Manning," she barked, obviously irritated by the interruption.

She rolled her eyes as she listened to the voice on the

other end of the phone. Then cursed beneath her breath. "All right. I'll be right there."

The publisher sighed heavily and shook her head. "I'm sorry, they want me on the ship. It seems they have a problem with the guest count. Dammit, George, I thought you were taking care of that." She sighed again. "Grace, Lucas, I'll see you both in a bit, at dinner.

"I'm so looking forward to hearing exciting tales of your previous bodyguard adventures, Lucas. If I can't get you on the cover of a book, perhaps we can think of a way to turn your true-life stories into a novel.

"Or better yet," she murmured, giving him another calculating perusal, "an autobiography. With you to promote it, the copies would literally leap off the shelves into women's shopping bags."

Before Lucas could assure her that he had no intention of entering the publishing business, she'd taken off with long, purposeful strides. They watched as she appeared to be giving the editorial director a tongue-lashing.

"The lady's not exactly going to win any awards for employer of the year," Lucas said.

"It appears George doesn't have the nerve to stand up to her," Grace said. "But I'd bet any slasher writer would love a glimpse into his fantasy life." She shook her head. "It's a shame, really. I've heard, through the grapevine, that he was very well thought of when he was heading up the diaper company. And Tina assured me, when the takeover first occurred, that he truly loves books. And was looking forward to marketing them."

"Now he's relegated to acting as pet-sitter to a cross-dressing mop of fur," Lucas murmured. "I gotta tell you, Gracie, darlin', you did choose one peculiar business." He smiled down at her. "So, do you want to run back to Sausalito before dinner?"

"Why would I want to do that?"

"To change clothes."

"Oh." The idea of racing across the bridge, then back again, just because her nemesis was about to show up in the same dress, seemed ludicrous. And unnecessary. Because just by showing up with Lucas, she'd already guaranteed that every writer, editor and agent on board would be watching them.

"No. It's not that big a deal."

"Especially since you look a damn sight better."

"You haven't even seen my competition yet."

"I don't have to. There's not a woman at this conference who can hold a candle to you, darlin'. Especially that skinny little beanpole, Bubbles."

Grace couldn't help giggling a little at that. "It's Buffy."

"Yeah. Right." He grinned down at her. "I'll have to keep that in mind. Wouldn't want to offend anyone."

She laughed again. Then, feeling incredibly light-hearted for someone who'd been receiving death threats, she found herself actually looking forward to the evening.

The cruise ship was as elaborate as a five-star hotel. The tables set up beside the huge windows were draped in white damask, and the banquettes and chairs were covered in ivory brocade. Candles flickered in antique silver holders in the center of the tables, and the light from the huge chandelier over the parquet dance floor bounced off sequins and crystal beads, splitting into rainbows that flashed like miniature strobe lights.

Champagne flowed, tuxedo-clad waiters rushed between tables and kitchen with silver trays laden with epicurean delights, and a mouth-watering array of pastries had been set up in towering tiers on the dessert table at one end of the dance floor. And if that wasn't enough to send even the most stalwart of chocoholics into endorphin overload, boxes of San Francisco's famed Ghiradelli chocolates had been placed on each table.

But Grace didn't need champagne to feel as if she was floating, didn't need any melt-in-the-mouth eclairs or chocolates to feel high. Just being with Lucas was enough to make her wish she could stop time right here and now. Even the murmur of an entire room of women when Buffy had arrived at the ship wearing the same frothy white gown Grace had paid a fortune for couldn't dampen her pleasure.

"You know," he murmured in her ear as they swayed together on the dance floor, "I think *I* should be paying *you* for this gig."

"Why?"

"This hardly feels like work." His hand pressed against the small of her back to hold her even closer. The feel of his muscular thighs against hers was enough to make Grace light-headed. For the first time in her life, she understood all too well why her heroines felt like swooning whenever they were in close proximity to the hero. "And I sure can't remember ever dancing with a client."

The British film star had wanted him to. Both vertically out on the dance floors of the mind-numbing number of clubs she'd dragged him to, and horizontally back at the hotel afterward. But that didn't count, since Lucas hadn't had any trouble turning her down.

"You're supposed to keep a close eye on me," Grace reminded him. As she tilted her head and looked up at him through her fringe of lashes, she realized she was actually flirting. Something she hadn't even realized she'd known how to do.

"No problem with that assignment." He chuckled and spun her around in a complex series of steps that made her feel like Ginger Rogers. "I'm not going to be putting in for hardship pay, that's for sure."

The song ended. He dipped her, bending her back over his arm so deeply that she was physically vulnerable and would have fallen if he suddenly released her. But Grace trusted him implicitly.

Their eyes met. And held, exchanging intimate messages too numerous and complex to catalog. Grace wasn't certain, but she thought her heart had ceased to beat as well. And she realized, on some distant level, that she was holding her breath.

They could have been the only two people in the room.

Lucas was the one to break the suspended spell. "This was a mistake." He pulled her back up and began shepherding her through the couples still crowded together on the dance floor.

"Dancing?"

"No. This damn cruise. I should have at least arranged to have a lifeboat ready so we could bail out of here." He shook his head. "I never realized until tonight exactly how long three hours could be."

She laughed at that and was amazed at the sultry sound coming from her lips. Where on earth had this siren come from? she wondered. "Poor darling. Didn't your grandmother Fancy ever teach you that patience was a virtue?"

"Yeah." His good mood restored, he flashed her that dazzling buccaneer's grin. "But I've never claimed to be a virtuous guy."

Even as she returned his smile, Grace knew that to be a lie. Lucas was the most honorable man she'd ever met. And the sexiest, which reminded her exactly how long it had been since he'd kissed her.

"It's getting a little stuffy in here," she murmured. "What would you say to taking a stroll around the deck?"

He rewarded her suggestion with another grin, more wicked and suggestive than the previous one. "Sweetheart, I thought you'd never ask."

The night was cool and foggy, making the lights of the

city look misty and romantic. In the distance, the lonely sound of foghorns tolled.

"You sure you want to do this?" he asked as the cold tendrils of fog wafted by like silent ghosts.

"Absolutely."

"As your bodyguard, it's my job to keep you safe. And well. I sure wouldn't want you getting a cold."

She fluttered her lashes, feeling amazingly like a sultry combination of Eve, Salome and Scarlett. Like every femme fatale ever born. She felt, Grace thought headily, like the kind of woman who could handle a man like Lucas Kincaid. The kind of woman who could wrap big strong heroes around her little finger.

"With you to keep me warm, I'll be fine. Besides, I wanted to get you out of there before Anne tries to drag you away. She's been eating you up with her greedy eyes all night."

The Queen of Romance had arrived at the last minute, resplendent in a black sequined halter top and a pencil thin leopard print crepe skirt slit nearly to her hip.

"Really? I hadn't noticed."

"She looked as if she's been starving her entire life and someone had declared you to be her own personal smorgasbord."

He chuckled, the sound rich and warm and too appealing for comfort. "If anyone's going to be taking a bite out of me, Gracie, darlin', it's you." He shrugged out of his black jacket and draped it over her bare shoulders. "Speaking of which…"

Leaning back against the damp railing, he pulled her into his arms and was about to kiss her when a voice called her name from out of the fog.

Muttering a curse beneath her breath, Grace turned and found herself face-to-face with Buffy, her husband-stealing ex-editor.

Buffy Cunningham Radcliffe was all the things Grace was not: petite, blond and, Grace reminded herself, treacherous and self-serving.

"Hello, Buffy." Grace gave the woman she'd once thought to be a friend her coolest smile. "Nice dress."

"I thought so when I saw it in the window at Saks." The former editor brushed a hand down the frothy skirt. "It appears we have similar taste in more than books."

"It appears so. Which is why, I suppose, you stole my husband."

"About that…" Buffy frowned and dragged her hand through her sleek honey bob. "We haven't had a chance to talk since your marriage broke up, Grace, and I feel I owe you an explanation—"

"Don't bother." Losing her husband didn't hurt now because it hadn't hurt then, Grace realized. Except for the blow to her pride. "Actually, Buffy, you're more than welcome to Robert. Quite honestly, I'd already written him off as one of those foolish youthful mistakes, like crocheted string bikinis and learning The Hustle."

"So you really don't have any feelings for Robert any longer?"

"None." Grace didn't even hate her former husband for his betrayal, because the sad fact was he wasn't worth the emotional energy. And never had been.

"I'm glad to hear that." If pauses could be pregnant, Grace decided this one had to be full term. "Then do you think there's a possibility you might be willing to collaborate with him again?" Buffy ventured tentatively.

"What?" Grace felt her jaw drop. "You can't be serious."

"I realize it may sound like an unusual arrangement, Grace, but if you'll just hear me out—"

"It's not just an unusual arrangement. It's impossible. Besides, Robert's and my working relationship was never a true collaboration. Because, in case you haven't noticed, Buffy, your husband can't write."

"Well, yes." Buffy swiped her hand through her hair again. Another diamond Grace's royalties had paid for flashed like a shooting star. "That appears to be the case. It's also why he—we—need you."

"I see. And what, exactly, would I get out of it?"

"Robert is a terrific promoter."

"Although no one asked my opinion, I'd think that Grace's work would pretty much promote itself," Lucas said.

"Well, yes. Of course it does," Buffy agreed quickly. "Grace is a wonderful writer. Probably the best in the business. But even great books need a little promotional push, especially when they first come out.

"You've never enjoyed appearing at conferences or book fairs, Grace. But Robert excels in being in the spotlight.

"And, of course, the fact that he's a man supposedly writing in a woman's genre garners even more press. The three of us had a very good partnership. It could be again."

Grace folded her arms across the beaded bodice of her Cinderella gown. "Not in this lifetime."

"You sound very firm about that."

Grace wondered if Buffy was really so stupid, or merely incredibly desperate. "My feet—and the rest of me—are set in concrete."

"I see." Buffy sighed and looked out over the water at the landmark Ghiradelli sign, which was barely visible in the bank of fog. "I told Robert that's what you'd say, but he insisted I give it the old college try." She paused, then turned back to Grace. "How are you and Tina getting along?"

"Fine. As always."

"I heard, through the grapevine, that there's a problem with your new contract."

"Oh?" Grace managed a bland expression even as she tried to figure out where this could have come from. "I wasn't aware of any problems. We're in negotiations, which seem to get more prolonged with each book, but I haven't any doubts we'll come to terms that will satisfy all sides."

"That's good to hear. So, I suppose this means you're not in the market for new representation?"

It was her second surprise of the evening. Grace couldn't decide whether Buffy was the most clueless individual she'd ever known, or the most desperate. "Are you actually suggesting I leave Tina and sign with you?"

"I was an editor at Penbrook for several years, Grace. I know the way they work, the way they think. I know all their little hot buttons. Whatever Tina's getting you, I can do better."

Grace went from surprised to flabbergasted. She couldn't imagine Buffy being so brazen as to even suggest such a thing. Then again, she'd never imagined her long-time editor would steal her husband, either. "You can't be serious."

"Look, Grace—" the former-editor-turned-agent put a hand on Grace's arm, her fingernails digging deep "—you have to understand, I'm in a bit of a bind here. Robert doesn't want me to take on any more clients because he feels they'd take my attention away from him—"

"That sounds familiar. Robert has always needed to be the center of attention."

"The problem is he can't write anything even remotely publishable. And I guess he's used to living on the Roberta Grace income, because he's been going through my credit cards like there's no tomorrow." She drew in a deep, shuddering breath. "To be perfectly honest, I'm at the end of my rope."

"Try putting it around his neck and throwing him off the pier," Grace suggested. "Look, Buffy, it's been interesting chatting with you, and I truly am sorry that everything has gone so badly for you. But I'm not the answer to your problems."

"You could be. If you gave up the Roberta Grace name."

"Why would I want to do that?"

"Perhaps because you owe me."

"I do?"

"I found you in the slush pile. I built your career." As if concerned at how bad that sounded, Buffy backtracked just a bit. "You're a wonderful writer, Grace." Her voice had gone from strident to soft and coaxing. "You could start over again without any problem."

Her fingers were locked around Grace's wrist like a handcuff. "If Robert had the rights to the Roberta Grace name," she continued, "we could hire someone to ghostwrite for him—"

"Someone like Anne Kilgallen?"

"Well, yes." Grace saw the guilty look flash in Buffy's blue eyes. "I take it you've spoken with Anne."

"Briefly. And needless to say, she mentioned it right away. And I'll tell you what I didn't bother to tell her.... Nothing's going to change my mind. Robert got a free ride for years, playing the part of the rich and famous male romance writer while I stayed home researching and writing the books.

"Now, I'll accept some of the blame for allowing that to happen, but that doesn't mean I'm giving up what I've worked so hard to achieve. I created the Roberta Grace name. And I'm keeping it."

She pried Buffy's steely grip loose. "And if you and

your husband have a problem with that, Buffy, then I guess I'll be seeing both of you in court."

That said, she turned and looked up at Lucas. "It seems to have gotten a bit crowded out here. Didn't they mention fireworks off the starboard side of the boat? Perhaps we could watch them from another deck."

"Sounds good to me." He nodded to Buffy, whose glare looked hot enough to melt diamonds.

"She doesn't seem real happy," he observed as they made their way to the metal stairs.

Grace shrugged. "She made her bed, she'll just have to lie in it." She didn't want to think about Buffy. Or Robert. Or any of them. She just wanted to enjoy this magical night with Lucas.

"Speaking of beds—" he pulled her into a dark corner and drew her into his arms "—how long did you say this boat ride was supposed to last?"

The lingering irritation left by her encounter with Buffy faded, like fog disappearing beneath a hot summer sun. Grace laughed and lifted her mouth for his kiss.

On the other side of the deck, Buffy Cunningham Radcliffe hunched against the cold, smoking a cigarette as she tried to calm her tattered nerves and soothe her whirling mind. Immersed as she was in her turmoiled thoughts, surrounded by the cold wet fog, which felt like icy fingers on her flesh, she failed to see the figure stealing up behind her.

There was a high-pitched whistling sound, followed by a thunderous boom as the promised fireworks exploded high in the sky over the bay.

Buffy heard the excited voices on the other side of the boat, which offered a better view. In no mood to enjoy the sight, she stayed where she was and tried to figure out how to salvage her faltering career.

A hand covered her mouth. Startled and frightened,

she began to fight, but her attacker had the element of surprise, along with the strength to lift her off her feet and throw her over the railing.

The sound of the former editor's body hitting water with a muffled splash was covered up by another explosion of red-white-and-blue fireworks.

Seconds later, the red glow of the abandoned cigarette arced through the air like a falling star, landing in the icy water, where it was instantly extinguished.

Grace and Lucas had returned to the dining salon after the fireworks when Robert came up to them. He seemed nervous, Lucas thought. And definitely distracted.

"Have you seen Buffy?"

"Don't tell me you've lost your bride already," Grace said flippantly.

"I don't need your sarcasm, Grace," he snapped. "I need to know where my agent is."

Grace thought the fact that he'd referred to Buffy as his agent rather than his wife spoke volumes about their relationship. "I have no idea. We had a brief conversation outside on the deck. But that was before the fireworks."

"Then she did speak with you?"

"As I said, only briefly."

"So, what do you think?"

"About what?"

"About collaborating again."

Grace had to laugh at that. Buffy and Robert made quite a pair; they obviously deserved each other. "I'll tell you the same thing I told your new agent, Robert. Not in this lifetime."

"Dammit, Grace. I'm making you a generous offer. There's a lot of money to be made with the Roberta Grace name—"

"You should know, since you were so good at spending it."

"Lord, you can be frustrating." He raked a hand through his blond hair. "Did you ever think that Geraldine might try to keep the name for Penbrook? And just get someone else to write the books? Some has-been desperate to resuscitate a dying career?"

"Someone like Anne?" Grace admittedly hadn't thought of that possibility before the conference. But since talking with the self-proclaimed Queen of Romance, she'd been forced to wonder.

"Rumor has it that she's at the top of Geraldine's list. It's not fair, Grace. We worked damn hard to build that name into a household word. How can you even consider walking away from it?"

"I'm not. I intend to win in court. Against you, and if it comes to that, against Geraldine. And Anne."

"Talk about your David and Goliath scenarios," he muttered. "Dammit, Grace…"

Grace wasn't certain exactly what happened next. All she knew was that Robert had reached out and taken hold of her shoulders, as if to shake some sense into her, when he was suddenly flying through the air. He landed, face first, in the center of the dessert table, scattering tarts and petits fours and breaking the towering ice-sculpture swan into splinters.

10

"OH, THAT WAS MARVELOUS," Jamie, who'd come up just in time to witness the event, declared with evil glee. "I only wish I'd had my video camera going—I could have undoubtedly paid for a new nursery with proceeds from selling copies of the tape."

There was no hint of an answering smile on Lucas's stony face. "Do me a favor and stay with Grace for a second," he said. "I've got one more thing to do."

"I won't let her out of my sight," Jamie promised.

"Lucas…" Grace said, demurring at the same time. Although she couldn't deny that seeing Robert the Rat sprawled amidst all those gooey pastries was more than a little enjoyable, neither did she want to be responsible for Lucas committing murder. Which he looked perfectly capable of doing.

"Don't worry." The reassuring words were ground out on a steely tone that Grace didn't find all that encouraging. "I won't kill him. Though the idea is tempting."

Too tempting, Lucas thought as he made his way through the crowd, which parted for him like the waters of the Red Sea. He stood over Grace's former husband, his hands curled into fists.

Robert dragged a hand down his face, leaving a messy trail of whipping cream and chocolate sauce. He glared up at his attacker. "The minute this ship docks, I'm going to call the police and press charges for assault and battery."

"You do that." Lucas leaned down, grabbed a fistful of stained shirt and yanked him back onto his feet, hauling him forward until their faces were inches apart. "In fact, why don't we give the D.A. a few more charges to prosecute? Like me throwing you overboard and leaving you to drown."

Aware that all eyes in the huge dining room were on him, Robert tried to bluster. "You wouldn't dare—"

"Want to bet? The only problem is the sharks probably wouldn't eat you. Professional courtesy being what it is."

"You had no right—"

"I had every right. In fact, see this?" He moved his jacket aside just enough to allow Robert to view the 9mm pistol in its shoulder holster. "Give me one reason why I shouldn't use it to shoot you for laying hands on my woman."

Before Robert could come up with an answer, the captain's voice came over the loudspeaker, announcing the ship's return to port.

"Looks as if tonight's your lucky night, Radcliffe, because I've just decided you're too much of a weasel to do hard time for." Lucas abruptly released the other man and watched as he fell back into the scattered, smashed pastries. "Touch Grace again and I won't be so generous."

With that threat hanging in the air between them, Lucas turned and walked back to Grace.

"My hero," Jamie said with a dramatic sigh, patting the front of her scarlet silk maternity dress.

He flashed a grin that was like the sun coming from behind gunmetal gray clouds. "Just doin' my job." He put his hand on Grace's waist and smiled down at her as if nothing out of the ordinary had happened. "Ready to leave, Gracie?"

"I think that might be a good idea," she murmured, glancing back at Robert, who was glaring at Lucas's back.

They were halfway down the gangplank when Geraldine caught up with them. "That was quite something," she said. "I have a feeling that this year's Penbrook Press party will go down in romance publishing history."

"You can bill me for the cost of the table," Lucas said. He was in no mood to listen to any complaints. He just wanted to escape this circus and get across the bay to his boat, where things were a great deal more quiet. And sane.

"Oh, I have no intention of doing that," Geraldine assured him. "That little display of macho heroics undoubtedly proved worlds more entertaining than the male strippers I'd considered hiring."

To Lucas's amazement, she touched a hand to his chest, in that same seductive way the British actress had when trying to convince him to try out the oversize Jacuzzi in her hotel room suite.

"You've no idea what a relief it is to know that our Grace is in such good hands. Isn't that true, Georgie?" she asked the man standing in his usual position right behind her.

"A relief," he agreed. For the first time since Lucas had met the editorial director, he wasn't carrying that damn dog. Lucas wondered idly if good old Georgie had finally shown some guts and dared to toss the Lhasa apso overboard. "It would be absolutely horrendous if any harm came to Rainbow Romances' beloved Roberta Grace."

"Speaking of my career with Rainbow Romances," Grace said, "I was talking with Buffy earlier, and she mentioned something that Anne Kilgallen had brought up this morning—"

"Oh, darling," Geraldine interrupted, as if sensing the

direction the conversation was about to take, "this is hardly the time or place to discuss business.

"Why don't you have Tina call me when we all get back to New York. We can have a lovely, ridiculously expensive lunch at the Plaza and talk tactics."

Grace decided that this wasn't really a hill to die on. Although she'd prefer to get matters settled, out of the corner of her eye she saw Robert stumbling to his feet. While she didn't think him foolhardy enough to take Lucas on again, she also didn't want to risk spending the rest of the night at the police station.

"All right. I'll do that." She exchanged nods with Geraldine and George, hugs with Jamie, then finally, she and Lucas were back in the Porsche, headed out of the city.

"Well, Geraldine's right about one thing," Grace decided as they crossed the bridge.

"What's that?"

"This was definitely the most exciting publisher's party I've ever attended. With the exception of that little fracas at the ABA a few years ago."

"Fracas?" Lucas checked the rearview mirror as he had the last time they'd driven to Sausalito, satisfied that once again they weren't being tailed.

"A bookseller had a bit too much merlot at lunch and made the mistake of asking a former heavyweight boxing champion infamous for settling personal disputes with his fists if he could actually read the autobiography he was signing.

"It took two hours to put the publisher's booth back together, and the bookseller ended up being taken to the hospital with a broken jaw and several cracked ribs."

"Dangerous business you've got yourself in, Gracie."

"So I'm discovering, the hard way."

"I suppose this is where I should apologize," he said.

"Apologize?"

"For punching out your ex."

He'd worried Grace might be annoyed at him for creating a scene. But her light laughter said otherwise. "You don't owe me an apology, Lucas. In fact, the sight of Robert sprawled amidst all those petits fours is going to be one of those things I'm still going to be smiling about when I'm an old lady."

"When you're sitting on the deck of our sailboat off some tropical island drinking *mai tais* after making love to your horny old husband."

"Now there's a thought," she murmured.

Lucas took it as encouragement that she didn't argue, and decided not to press his luck. "Do you want to talk about this latest glitch?" he asked. "About the possibility of Penbrook keeping your name?"

Grace was surprised and pleased that he was inviting her to fret about business when she knew that his original plans for the rest of the evening had centered around pleasure.

"I think I'll wait until tomorrow to start obsessing over that one. I don't want to think about business, or Robert or Tina or Geraldine." She placed her hand on his thigh. "I just want to dwell in the moment."

He covered her hand with his. "Now there's a plan." His pirate's grin was a wicked slash of white that made her body—and her heart—yearn.

Neither Lucas nor Grace said anything the rest of the way to Sausalito. There was no need.

The thick fog created a muffler, making Grace feel as if she and Lucas were the only two people in the world as they walked hand in hand down the dock to the *Rebel's Reward*. Although she certainly wasn't the type of woman to fall into bed with a man she'd just met—in fact, Robert had been the only other man she had ever slept with—what they were about to do felt amazingly right.

"I was thinking," Lucas murmured as he helped her onto the deck. "Perhaps I'm being selfish."

"Selfish?"

"Well, I suppose, technically, I might be accused of rushing you into things."

"I suppose that's true," she agreed as he unlocked the door that led belowdecks. "Technically." In contrast to the cool night air, the cabin was warm and cozy. She was even warmer; in fact, Grace felt as if she were burning from the inside out.

"I don't want you to feel pressured because of any misplaced idea of gratitude."

She shrugged out of the tuxedo jacket she'd been wearing since they left the boat. Her bare shoulders gleamed like alabaster in the low lamplight, but looked much, much softer. It made him ache for a taste. Until meeting Grace, Lucas had never known that hunger had claws. *Patience*, he reminded himself as he dispensed with his shoulder holster and pistol.

"Nothing's going to happen here tonight unless you want it to."

"I know. And I appreciate that." The filmy stole that teased more than it covered joined the jacket on the back of the chair. "Then again," she considered, "as you've pointed out, it's undoubtedly foolhardy to reject a gift from the gods."

Because he was desperate to touch her, Lucas stayed where he was, giving her room to maneuver, time to decide. "I want you to be very, very sure about this, Grace."

His dark eyes were as solemn as his tone. The fact that he'd called her Grace, rather than the more familiar Gracie, assured her that Lucas was very serious.

"I am." It was barely a whisper, hardly audible over the faint slapping of water against the hull of the ketch.

"Because if I make love to you tonight, I'm not going to be willing to let you go."

"So much for the three-night stand." Her attempt at humor fell decidedly flat.

"Three nights isn't bad for a start. But I want a lot more."

Grace told herself that some women—most women—would think she was crazy for even hesitating. But her independence had been a hard-won prize, and she worried that if she allowed herself to love and be loved by such a strong-willed man, she might end up losing all she'd gained.

"You don't have to worry about things being like they were with your ex," he said, once again seeming to possess the uncanny ability to read her mind. "My ego is comfortable enough to appreciate your strengths. As well as your soft spots."

Because he could no longer resist touching her, he gathered her into his arms. "And speaking of soft spots..." he murmured, nuzzling her neck.

She wrapped her arms around him and held on hard. "I hate to admit this," she muttered into his shirt, "but since we're being totally honest here, I think I should tell you I'm a little bit afraid."

Damn. It was the last thing he wanted. Lucas decided her reaction was what he got for belting her ex-husband. She'd already been married to a man who'd mentally abused her; it only made sense that she'd be nervous about getting involved with a gun-toting brute who solved problems with his fists.

He cupped her chin in his fingers, as delicately as if he were holding spun glass, and lifted her gaze to his. Her eyes were the deep green of the sea. They were also laced with an anxiety that made him want to go out and drown himself in the bay.

"I'd never hurt you, Grace."

Those remarkable eyes widened with obvious surprise. "I know that, Lucas."

Relief flowed through him like a cool, clear river. "I thought, perhaps, because of what I did to the Rat—"

"No." She pressed her fingers against his lips, forestalling his words. "We're not going to talk about him. Not tonight." She touched her palm to Lucas's cheek. "What I'm afraid of is disappointing you."

"Oh, baby." He took hold of her wrist, turned his head and pressed a kiss against the sensitive flesh of her palm, sending a jolt of heat radiating outward through the rest of her body. "If there's one thing you could never do it's disappoint me."

It was so easy. Amazingly easy. As he lifted her into his arms and carried her into the adjoining stateroom, Grace felt as if she'd been waiting for years for this moment. Which she had, she realized as he put her back on her feet beside the bed, releasing her long enough to light the gas fire. She'd been waiting her entire life for this man.

The flames came instantly to life, creating a flare of heat and a flickering glow that danced on the walls. The shutters were closed, ensuring privacy, although she suspected that the fog that had curled around the ketch like a sleepy gray cat would have prevented anyone from seeing into the cabin.

"You are so beautiful."

With his eyes on hers, he unzipped her gown. It drifted to the floor in a frothy white cloud. With any other man she might have felt self-conscious, standing there wearing only a strapless bra, tummy-control panty hose and a pair of ridiculously expensive lace bikini panties she'd splurged on from the Victoria's Secret catalog. But not with Lucas. Never with Lucas. The way he was looking at her made Grace feel like the most beautiful woman in the world.

"So are you." Turnabout being fair play, she tugged at his tie, tossed it onto the built-in dresser, then went to work on the ebony studs running down the front of his pleated shirt. "Whoever invented these things was a sadist," she complained, as her fingers seemed to turn to stone.

He chuckled and pressed a kiss atop her bent head. "Take your time. We've all night." And thousands more, if he had anything to say about it.

There was a bit more fumbling, then finally, just when her nerves were at the breaking point—success! She folded back the shirt and pushed it off his shoulders, only to be met with another obstruction. "I can't believe this!"

"Here. Let me help." He unfastened the cuff links. "Free at last."

"Thank God." She pulled the shirt the rest of the way off and tossed it uncaringly onto the floor beside her discarded gown. Her hands explored smooth tanned skin, taut muscles and a frightening ridge of raised white scar that ran from his right nipple nearly to his navel. A frisson of ice skipped up her spine. "What's this?"

"Just an old knife wound." Her touch was magic. Torment. Lucas forced a careless shrug when his body wanted to tremble. "A souvenir of a past assignment that didn't go exactly as planned."

"My God, if that had been on the other side, it could have ripped open your heart."

"I've always been lucky."

Because thinking about that night wasn't his favorite thing to do at any time, but least of all when he was about to bed the woman he'd been waiting for all his life, Lucas framed her face between his hands and kissed her. Hard.

Rocked by the power and greed of Lucas's mouth,

Grace dragged her hand through his hair, ripping away the black cord, tangling her fists in the long ebony silk that was the only soft thing about this man. Tongues tangled as he savaged her mouth. She drew in a sharp breath as he yanked down the snowy bra and closed his hands over her breasts.

"I want…" Her head was flung back, her body arched like a tautly strung bow. "I need…"

She couldn't speak. Couldn't think. The need for him was pulsing between her thighs.

"I know." When he shoved a hand into the front of the panty hose, cupping her in that place where a hundred, a thousand, pulse points hummed, air clogged thickly in her lungs.

"You're so hot." His fingers glided through the silken curls. "So wet." He slipped a finger into her dampness, swallowing her soft moan beneath his mouth. "So ready for me." Another finger followed, stretching her, plunging deep.

As the warm moisture flowed over his hand like melted honey, Lucas experienced a new level of lust. She was whimpering now, helpless, vulnerable, willing to go anywhere he took her.

"Lucas…" She pressed her thighs tightly together, capturing his hand between her legs, squirming against the intimate touch. "Please…"

He'd dreamed of her like this. Hot and hungry and his. But he was rapidly discovering that the dreams hadn't approached reality.

"Yes," he said, his breath warm on her parted lips. He scraped a callused thumb against her ultrasensitive spot. "Now."

Helpless against the unspeakable, unmanageable pleasure washing over her, Grace came with a wild, gasping sob. She clung to him, her nails digging half-moon-shaped gouges into his shoulders as her body seemed to dissolve.

"Oh!" She was gasping, breathless and as limp as melted wax. "That was...amazing."

"Amazing." She was trembling. Lucas held her close while the aftermath of her violent climax continued to pulse through her body.

He'd never met a woman as generous, as trusting as Grace. She'd opened for him fully, holding nothing back, making him feel as powerful as an ancient pagan god. And as humble as a penitent. "You're amazing." He kissed her cheek. Her temple, her eyelids, her lips.

"Not me." Her lids fluttered open, her gaze still a little unfocused, but as sober as he'd ever seen it. "It's us." Her hand felt strangely heavy as she lifted it to his face. His beautiful, scarred pirate's face. "Us together."

He'd known they'd be good together. But even Lucas, with all his experience, hadn't begun to imagine how good. "And just think," he said with a rough, husky laugh as he pulled her down onto the bed. "We've just begun."

It had started to rain. The steady tap tap tap on the deck above them added a counterpoint to the soft sighs and faint moans. Desire heightened. Breaths quickened as the rest of their clothes were ripped away.

The room radiated with a heat that had nothing to do with the flickering gas fire. His hands and lips were at times so gentle Grace almost wept. Then, just as she felt herself sinking into the luxurious sensations, they'd turn so rough and thrilling that emotions tangled and heightened feelings came tumbling over each other, making her almost faint from desire.

He did things to her, with her, that Grace had never imagined, and still left her begging for more. His mouth explored every curve and crevice. He feasted on her, his tongue plunging deep into her molten center, teeth nipping at tingling pink flesh, bringing her to countless orgasms. And just when she was certain there couldn't be more, that she couldn't take another moment of these devastating, dizzying sensations, he'd bend her body in some new possessive way and insist that he wasn't finished. That she hadn't had enough. Yet.

Grace felt absolutely wanton, stunned and thrilled by lascivious appetites she'd never known were lurking deep inside her. Yet even as she submitted to Lucas's primal demands, she never felt as if she were surrendering. Because as his flesh burned and his breath grew rough and labored and his body became engorged with need—for her!—Grace experienced absolute female power.

Locked together, they rolled over the bed, tangling sheets, sending pillows falling onto the floor. Lucas's teeth scraped against a nipple, drawing a gasp, then, before Grace had stopped trembling, they were biting at the distended nub between her slick, quaking thighs.

Lucas wanted her. In every way a man could want a woman he'd fallen in love with. He wanted to pleasure Grace as he'd never pleasured any other woman. Wanted her to experience sensations she'd never felt with any other man. He wanted to possess her—body, mind and soul.

Although he was approaching desperation, he took the necessary time to protect her. Then moved between her thighs, hot male flesh resting against hot female flesh.

"Look at me."

Shuddering with sexual anticipation, Grace did as he commanded.

Although he was aching to plunge into her, he paused to drink in the sight of her flesh glowing in the flickering firelight, her ravished, swollen lips, her eyes dazed, almost blind.

"I want to watch you," he murmured as he tilted his hips forward, separating the rosy pink folds with the tip of his sex. "I want to watch your eyes when I take you over the edge."

She blinked slowly, almost hypnotically, as if in an attempt to clear her vision. "Oh, yes."

He didn't need a second invitation. He cupped her hips, lifted them off the mattress and surged into her, filling her, claiming her. Loving her.

His thrusts were deep and slow, and utterly ruthless. Grace's hands clawed at the sheets as he drove them both into the smoke. Caught up in a breathless, burning need, she struggled to fill her scorched lungs with air.

She heard Lucas moan, felt him stiffen. And then, as his mouth captured hers again, he dragged them both into the flames.

LUCAS HELD HER close long after their breathing steadied, the tremors had ceased and their bodies had cooled.

"Are we alive?" Grace asked, when she could finally talk again.

"I think so." He touched his mouth to hers. "Definitely. But I'm not certain about the rest of the bay area, because if that wasn't an earthquake, we've just logged in a personal best."

She laughed lightly at that and snuggled against him, loving the way he could make her burn one moment, then feel so amazingly lighthearted the next. She'd never laughed in bed, although there'd been more than one occasion when she'd wanted to cry.

She trailed a lazy finger down his chest and, since she was feeling happier than she'd ever felt in her life, tried not to think about how he'd gotten that terrible scar. His flesh was no longer hot to the touch, but wonderfully warm and moist, emanating a musky scent that, amazingly, stimulated another little spike of desire.

"I made you sweat."

"You did a lot more than that, Gracie, darlin'." He combed lazy fingers through her tousled caramel hair. "You damn near killed me."

"I never knew it could be like that." She pressed her lips against his stomach and felt his muscles clench and his sharp intake of breath. "I never knew I could be like that."

"I knew." The erotic touch of her open mouth was all it took to make him hard again. "The minute I first saw you, I knew that you'd be hot."

"Hot." She lifted her head, her eyes gleaming with a dangerous, sultry feminine pride that brought to mind how Delilah must have looked, right before she decided to give Samson that haircut. "I was, wasn't I? Hot and sexy." She rolled over on top of him, chest-to-chest, thigh-to-thigh and, Lord help him, sex-to-sex.

"The hottest, sexiest, most desirable woman on the planet," he managed to say in a strangled voice as she began moving against him in a way designed to rekindle smoldering ashes. "Hell, the entire universe."

"I know." Her laugh, throaty with self-satisfaction, bubbled up from deep inside her. "And I love it."

Without taking her eyes from his, she reached into the drawer of the bedside table, locating the foil package on the first try. "How many of these do we have?" she asked as she ripped it open.

"I don't know." He couldn't think, could barely speak as her fingers smoothed the condom over throbbing flesh. "I suppose a half dozen or so."

"A half dozen." She leaned forward again, the diamond-hard tips of her breasts brushing against his chest as she touched her smiling lips to his. "I suppose that will do." Her tongue made a wet swathe along the seam of his mouth; her perfect white teeth nibbled at his lower lip. "For starters."

"I think I've created a monster." He made a ragged sound that was half groan, half laugh. "What if I can't live up to your expectations?"

"Don't worry, Lucas." She smiled down at him as she took him deep into her welcoming warmth. "I'll help you."

"Well then," he said, as she began to rock her hips in a slow, tantalizing rhythm, "I guess we shouldn't have any problem."

Her lips curved; her eyes sparkled emerald bright with passion and with humor. "That's exactly what I was thinking."

IT WAS THE SCREAM that woke her. A scream that chilled her blood and had her leaping out of bed. Grace's heart was pounding so hard and so fast she wondered if it was possible for a twenty-seven-year-old woman to have a heart attack.

Disoriented from fear and the unfamiliar surroundings, it took a moment for Grace to realize where she was. Then she saw Lucas, sitting bolt upright in bed, and realized he'd made that agonizingly pained sound.

"Lucas." She returned to the bed. "Wake up." He was soaking wet and shaking. Whatever nightmare had gripped his mind must be horrific. His eyes were open, but she suspected he wasn't seeing the cozy stateroom, but something much, much more deadly.

"You're dreaming." She held his head against her breasts and stroked his damp hair from his forehead. "It's all right." Her hands skimmed down his back. "It's only a nightmare."

Grace nearly wept with relief when he looked up and his dark eyes slowly revealed that he'd returned to her.

"Hell." He dragged an unsteady hand through his hair. "I'm sorry, Grace. I must have scared you to death."

"Only for a moment. Actually, I was more worried about you."

He closed his eyes and leaned back against the wooden headboard. "I haven't had that nightmare since I quit drinking.... Dammit!"

"Maybe if you talk about it…" she suggested quietly.

"Yeah, that's the way to show a lady a good time. Bed her, then terrify her half out of her wits. With a technique like this, it's a wonder I don't have to beat the women off with a stick."

Accustomed to his cocky male ego, Grace was surprised and more than a little moved by his apparent self-loathing.

"News flash, Kincaid," she said. "I never expected you to leap over tall buildings in a single bound. Personally, Superman never appealed to me. I much prefer Batman. He has more shadows, more vulnerabilities."

Lucas would have expected, at the very least, distress. Perhaps revulsion. Or even worse, pity. Her matter-of-fact attitude only made him love her more.

"You realize, of course, that you may actually be as crazy as me?" he murmured.

"Perhaps." He watched the pleasure wipe out the concern that had been written across her face. Her lovely, lovely face. "I suppose that's why we're so good together." She leaned forward and touched her smiling mouth to his.

The kiss was slow and sweet. Lucas could have kissed her forever. Unfortunately, Grace had something else in mind.

"I'd really like to know what happened to you," she

said softly. "What it was that made you quit the service, that made you drink and has you waking up in a cold sweat."

Lucas figured that if he wanted to spend a lifetime with Grace, he owed her the truth. She deserved to know what kind of man he was. What kind he'd been. "You know I was in the navy."

"Yes."

"I was a SEAL. Do you know what that is?"

"Sort of. It's like the Army's Special Forces, right?"

"Right." He put his arm around her shoulder and remembered that night—remembered wading through the frothy foam at the edge of the sea beneath a silver sickle of a moon that was barely visible through the thick gray fog.

The tide had been ebbing from the deserted beach, leaving broken seashells that could crunch underfoot if he'd mistakenly stepped on them. The hard-packed sand, which had sparkled like sugar beneath the hot tropical sun only hours earlier, appeared a dull charcoal gray somewhere between the pewter of the fog and the black of the sea.

Lucas shook off the too-clear vision. "We'd go in where angels and sane men are sensible enough not to tread."

He'd known from the beginning that a single mistake could get him killed. If he was forced to be completely honest, he'd have to admit that was part of the appeal. Although he'd never done drugs, Lucas had often suspected there wasn't a drug made that could begin to equal the adrenaline rush that came with putting your life on the line.

"We marked targets for artillery and bombers, took out radar on occasion, did some covert intelligence—"

"You were a spy?"

"Don't let your writer's imagination run away with you. It's not like James Bond."

"So you say." She smiled and snuggled up against him. "But you'll never convince me. Don't forget, I've seen you in a tux."

He shook his head. "Let me put it another way. You know how mothers like to brag about their kids?"

"Of course. Mine certainly does."

"Well, my mom once told me that although she was proud of me, I made that a little difficult."

"Why?"

"Because at cocktail parties, when all the other mothers were boasting about their doctor or lawyer sons and daughters, she didn't feel comfortable telling everyone about her son, the assassin."

He felt Grace go still for a suspended moment. Felt the goose bumps rise on her arms. And waited.

"I suppose I can understand that," she said finally. Slowly. "But I also suppose that those of us who are fortunate enough to go our entire lives without having to face such situations should be grateful that others are willing to risk their lives to keep us safe."

It occurred to him that this was almost too easy.

And Lucas had never trusted anything easy.

"I don't think you get it, Grace. The man you're in bed with is a man who's killed. A man some, even my own mother, might call a professional assassin. And, although I've never actually defined myself that way, and certainly never received any pleasure in taking a life, if necessary, I'd do it again." Like in order to keep her safe, he thought, but did not say. "The trick was to keep the guys on the other side from killing me."

His words, spoken as a warning, did not seem to change her mind. Grace lifted a hand to his cheek. "I'm glad you were so good at your job that they weren't able to do that. Otherwise, we never would have met. Never would have..." She paused as she realized she was about to say *fallen in love*. "Been here like this," she said instead.

Deeply humbled, and vastly grateful, Lucas lowered his forehead to hers.

"You really are an incredible woman, Gracie."

She tilted her head back and looked up at him, her heart in her eyes. "I want to hear what happened," she insisted quietly. "Because I care for you. And then, sailor, you're going to get very, very lucky."

"I already am." He'd never meant anything more.

Her pleased laugh was as soft as the hand warming his face. "Another thing we have in common."

Censoring the story a bit to protect his ego and her sensibilities, Lucas gave her the bare-bones version. How he'd been sent to the remote Caribbean island in order to confirm a rumor about a conference between a faction of the Russian mafia and a South American drug lord.

"The deal was simple enough, as such things go," he said. "The Russians, mostly former soldiers in the Soviet army, had arms for sale, while members of the cartel were willing to trade drugs for high-tech military weapons."

"Drugs that could earn a tidy profit when cut and sold on the world market," Grace guessed. Coincidentally, she remembered Jamie writing a romantic suspense novel based on a similar scenario.

"Exactly. I was never sure how many agencies had a piece of the action. Naval Intelligence, obviously. The CIA, DEA, Interpol, at the very least. I also knew going in that if the mission became public, every one of those organizations would deny my existence."

"That's horrible!"

Lucas shrugged. "That's just the way things work. I'd always liked being on my own." He dragged a hand down his face as he thought back to that night. "But then again, I'd never screwed up before, either."

He recalled all too well how he'd been heading for the lush green cliff when the entire beach lit up as if a thousand suns had just turned on. When his eyes had adjusted to the blinding glare, he'd seen that the beach was no longer deserted and had realized that this was the night his luck had finally run out.

"What went wrong?"

"It turned out that they had a man on the inside. A naval officer who'd been living beyond his income and decided to sell a few government secrets. But I didn't know that at the time."

Finding a live hostage more valuable than a dead naval officer, they hadn't killed him. But as days turned into weeks, Lucas discovered that the torture techniques he'd been taught about during SEAL training were not exaggerated. Again, to protect her, Lucas opted not to tell Grace how, after six weeks as a hostage, he'd no longer cared if his captors killed him or not.

"I managed to hone a knife of sorts out of a shell and was prepared to take out as many of them as I could," he continued, "when a crack rescue squad, led by a SEAL pal of mine, showed up in the nick of time, just like the cavalry in the old westerns. The team broke into the compound, created general mayhem, then airlifted me out by helicopter.

"I spent some time in the hospital. Then, after I got out, I kept rerunning that night in my mind, trying to think what I could have done differently. I started drinking to blank the memories out so I could sleep, which was when things really began to go downhill." Lucas knew that even Grace's generous heart probably wouldn't have wanted anything to do with him during those lost months.

Silence pooled around them; there was only the continued sound of the rain on the roof, the muffled moan of the ropes rubbing against the dock, the haunting, lonely sound of foghorns out in the bay.

"What happened to the traitor?" she asked finally. "The naval officer who was responsible for you being captured?"

"Seems the guilt must have gotten to him, or else he couldn't take the idea of spending the rest of his life in a federal prison, because he was found dead in his San Diego condo. He'd been shot with his own gun. The autopsy concluded it was suicide."

Lucas waited for her to question that statement. As he had himself on more than one occasion. The web of secrecy was a wide and tangled one; he could well imagine that people higher up than he might have thought one more death was a practical way of handling the potentially embarrassing situation.

Again, Grace surprised him.

"I'm glad he's dead," she decided.

"Me, too." The rush of relief was like standing beneath a crystal waterfall. For the first time in years, Lucas felt clean. "And you really are incredible…. So, is it time for me to get lucky?"

"Absolutely."

The dark, solemn mood lifted. Laughing again, Grace threw her arms around Lucas's neck, covered his mouth with hers and spent the rest of the long, love-filled night showing him exactly how incredible she could be.

11

IT HAD STOPPED RAINING and a bright July sun was streaming through the window when Grace woke up. She was alone in the stateroom, and a glance at the bedside clock radio told her it was almost noon. Having always been an early riser, she was amazed that she'd slept so late. But then again, she considered, as she climbed out of the high bed, by the time she'd finally drifted off to sleep in Lucas's arms, the pearlescent light of a new day had already been filtering into the cabin through the slats of the blinds.

She showered quickly, threw on a pair of shorts and a T-shirt and sneakers, and went to find Lucas.

He was in the galley, the laptop computer on the table, the modem plugged into a phone jack.

"Good morning." He rose and poured her a cup of coffee from the carafe. "How did you sleep?"

"Like the dead." The irony of that statement, considering the circumstances, struck home. "I mean well," she amended. "I slept amazingly well." Which had been all the more surprising since she'd always been one of those people who never adapted to strange beds.

"It's the water." He handed her the earthenware mug. "It rocks you like a cradle. You can't help but sleep like a baby."

"Perhaps." She took a sip of the French roast coffee and willed the caffeine to click in. "Then again, it could be all the exercise I had last night."

"There is that," he agreed in that smooth drawl that never failed to slip beneath her skin. "Would you like some breakfast? I've got some cinnamon rolls, or if you're hungry, I can make bacon and eggs or pancakes."

"No, thank you." Before she'd met Lucas, Grace had never in her entire life had a man cook for her. She thought it ironic that the most masculine male she'd ever met would be the one to offer. "It's so late, I think I'll just wait for lunch."

"Your call," he said agreeably, then sat back down at the table and began moving his fingers across the compact computer keyboard again. "Damn."

"What?" Grace, who'd been watching a boat berthed nearby head away from the dock, turned back toward him.

"I forgot something." He stood up again, brushed his hands through her hair, which she'd left loose this morning, and lowered his mouth to hers.

The kiss was short, sweet and devastatingly potent. As she plunged straight into it, needs rose inside her like a blazing sun rising out of cool waters. Her head was still whirling when he released her.

"That's better." Lucas drank in the sight of her flushed cheeks, her unfocused eyes. Satisfied, at least for now, he resisted scooping her up and carrying her back to bed. "Lord, you really are amazing, Gracie."

"You're not so bad yourself, sailor."

They shared a laugh. Another quick, friendly kiss. "Mind if I work a little before we go back to the city?" he asked. "I've almost got it buttoned up."

"Not at all." If she were to be absolutely honest, Grace would have to admit that she didn't care if she ever returned to the city. Or, more particularly, the conference.

As she strolled around the galley and adjoining main salon, examining the bits and pieces Lucas had obviously picked up on various sailing expeditions—a piece of drift-wood shaped like a dolphin, a scattering of shells in a brass bowl from the Orient, an antique sextant—it dawned on Grace that she wasn't suffering from any un-comfortable morning-after feelings.

On the contrary, being with Lucas this way seemed strangely right. In fact, it felt almost perfect, she mused as she sipped the coffee and watched the white sails skim-ming across the bay toward the bridge and the city. Or would be if it weren't for the little matter of someone wanting to kill her.

"What are you working on?" She came back to the gal-ley and stood behind him.

"A hunch."

She leaned over his shoulder. "It looks like a bank state-ment."

"That's precisely what it is."

"Whose?"

"Jamie Winston's."

"Jamie's?" Grace stared at him. "You hacked your way into my best friend's personal bank account?"

"Yeah."

The fact that he seemed so matter-of-fact about such subterfuge made a temper she'd never known she pos-sessed flare. "I can't believe it!" She rubbed at her temple as she began to pace. "Not only is it a horrible betrayal of someone I care about deeply—someone who cares about me—what right do you have to break the law like that?"

"I was hired to keep you safe. And I'll break every damn law on the books to do that."

His expression revealed not an iota of guilt; his voice was absolutely reasonable. Grace reminded herself that he'd been a spy. An assassin. Obviously, after all he'd done, he wasn't going to take a little hacking very seri-ously.

"You were hired as a bodyguard," she stated. "You're not a detective."

"True enough. But didn't anyone ever tell you that knowledge is power, Gracie?"

"You're not taking this seriously."

"On the contrary. I take it very seriously. Because I take *you* seriously."

His quiet voice took a bit of the wind out of her sails. There was nothing she could say to that. She tilted her head and studied him. He was a man who lived by his own rules. If she were to allow herself to love him, she'd have to accept that part of him, just as she'd already accepted his past.

"I've never really believed in the ends justifying the means."

"Now why doesn't that surprise me?"

Another silence stretched between them. Lucas seemed more than willing to wait until doomsday for her to make a decision.

Grace decided that the best thing to do would be just to say it straight out. "I need to know I can trust you."

She saw the flash of disappointment in his eyes, but he nodded, as if her concern had merit. "That's only reasonable. And all I can do is promise that although we got off to a rocky start, I'll never lie to you."

She was beginning to get a handle on how his mind worked. "How about keeping things from me?"

"Ah, what the good sisters at St. Cecilia's used to call a sin of omission."

"Exactly."

He thought about that for a minute. "That's a harder one."

It was her turn to wait.

"Okay," Lucas said finally, throwing up his hands,

both literally and figuratively. "You win. I won't keep anything I think you need to know—"

"Anything," she interjected.

He cursed and dragged his hand through his hair. "Whoever would have expected America's most beloved romance author to be so damn mule headed?"

She lifted her chin and met his hard, frustrated gaze straight on. "Believe me, it's coming as a surprise to me, as well."

They looked at each other over a gulf that seemed as wide and as deep as the Grand Canyon.

"Anything." Lucas finally ground out the promise through clenched teeth.

Grace's smile was warm and gracious. "Thank you, Lucas."

"You're welcome." He paused, trying to decide how to break this to her, then deciding it would best to tell her straight out. "Did you happen to know that your friend is in deep financial trouble?"

"What kind of trouble?"

"Her husband spent a lot of money setting up his office, which might not have been a problem if his mortgage, car payments and monthly expenses weren't based on his former salary at his high-powered law firm."

"But he received a generous payment for his partner's share," Grace said. "And Jamie said that some of his clients came with him to his new firm."

"True. But as I said, he has a lot of start-up expenses. And neither of them have ever been all that frugal. They've been living on charge cards the past six months, floating payments from one to the other, and it appears their house of platinum cards is about to crumble."

"I don't believe it!" Grace shook her head and sank into a chair. "Why didn't she tell me? I could have helped."

"Pride is a powerful thing," Lucas suggested.

"True. But we're best friends." A thought occurred to her. "This conference is not inexpensive. If they're in financial difficulties, why..." Her voice drifted off as the answer came. "She said she wouldn't miss seeing me win a ROMI. She spent money she didn't have to support me."

"Perhaps. Or perhaps she came here to try to work a deal with Geraldine Manning, in the event the Roberta Grace name ends up with Penbrook Press."

"She'd never do that," Grace said firmly. "I can't believe you'd even consider her a suspect."

"I consider everyone a suspect," he countered.

That idea made her more sad than angry. "That's a terrible way to live."

"Granted. Which is one more reason I'm getting out of the business. After we catch whoever it is who's out to kill you."

Grace caught his use of the word *we* and decided that while her newfound independence was all very well and good, there was definitely something to be said for being part of a team. What she didn't like was Lucas thinking that Jamie could actually want her dead. Or Tina. Or Geraldine. Or any of the two thousand other conference attendees.

"I hate this," she muttered.

"You're not the only one. But then again, I'm not going to bitch, since I wouldn't have met you if I hadn't taken the case. Which definitely proves the old adage about a silver lining. And now, since we've agreed to be so honest with one another, want me to show you what I found in Geraldine's personal account?"

For the next five minutes Grace watched as he pulled up the numbers showing three payments to Geraldine from the senior Dwyer. They'd been drawn on the

Dwyer's Diapers account and listed on those corporate books as bonuses.

"That's not so surprising," Grace argued. "Executives at her level often have bonus payments included in their income."

"Granted. But they don't show up anywhere on either Dwyer's or Penbrook Press's employee tax-withholding records."

"I don't understand."

"What we seem to have going for us here, Gracie, is some type of personal payoff. But I can't figure out what for." He did some more tapping and accessed Grace's royalty statement. "Then there's this little problem. I've tried to reconcile your print runs, the shipping numbers, the warehouse stock and the returns of books that didn't sell with what you've been paid in royalties, and it just doesn't add up."

"What do you mean?"

"There are a lot of books missing, Gracie."

"How many is a lot?"

"At least a hundred thousand. Give or take a few thousand."

"That many?" Grace sank down onto a chair. "How could that be?"

"Good question. At first I thought that Penbrook might be just cooking their books, but I checked out other writers' accounts, and they seem to be pretty much on the money, except for the random mistake translating payments from foreign sales into dollars."

Grace thought about that a moment. "Surely you don't think that Geraldine could be skimming from my sales?"

"That's what it looks like. Although that still doesn't explain the payments from George Senior."

Grace looked up at Lucas, her expression confused, her eyes distressed. "My last book stayed on all the lists longer than any of the previous ones, but my sales seemed to drop this spring royalty period."

"Was any mention made of that?"

"Actually, Tina told me that Geraldine was using the lower numbers to play hardball on these new contract negotiations. Since Penbrook wasn't the same place anymore, what with all the management changes, I was considering moving to another house. And although Geraldine talks a great line, telling me how much she loves my books, I have to admit I get the feeling that she isn't exactly going to bend over backward to convince me to stay."

"But you're their bestselling writer."

"I know." Grace dragged her hand through her hair. "But it's a subjective business. Perhaps Geraldine wants to change the type of book Rainbow Romances is publishing."

"Has she spoken to you or Tina about changing the focus of your stories?"

"No." She shook her head. "I can't believe Geraldine would do this to me. Admittedly, I don't much like her, or her way of doing business. But I've been with Penbrook for years, I've made a lot of money for the company. Why would she choose me to steal from?"

"For the same reason Willie Sutton robbed banks. Your books are where the money is. Your print runs are high enough that she probably figured she could get away with bleeding a few thousand bucks from the royalty account."

Grace sighed. Had it been less than an hour ago that she'd awakened feeling so happy? So positive? Right now, faced with the possibility of such betrayal, she felt as if it could have been a lifetime ago. "But surely she'd get caught."

"Perhaps. But if she forces you to go to another publisher, it'd probably never come out."

"I still don't understand," Grace complained. "If I'm their bestselling author, why wouldn't she want me to stay at Penbrook? After all, she's promised the stockholders that she'll boost profits. Isn't that going to be harder to do if I leave?"

"It would seem to me that it would," Lucas agreed. "But then again, Gracie, as we've agreed before, you're definitely working in one wacky business." He skimmed a hand down her hair, a casual gesture meant to soothe. "I suppose we'll have to ask the lady herself."

"I suppose so," Grace said with a decided lack of enthusiasm. Still, once again she couldn't deny that she liked the sound of that *we*.

"But just because she may be stealing from me doesn't necessarily mean Geraldine's the one trying to kill me."

"I never said she was," he reminded her.

But Grace knew, as the silence returned, that they were both thinking about the possibility of just such a thing.

"May I make a suggestion?" he asked.

"Of course."

"We can take you back to the city now, and get this over with before tonight's awards banquet. Or we can play hooky."

"Hooky?"

"The sun is shining, Gracie." His smile belied the seriousness of the subject they'd been discussing. "What would you say to coming sailing on the bay with me?"

It was, with the exception of making love, the best idea he'd come up with yet. Grace smiled back. "I'd say yes."

IT WAS HEAVEN. Grace had almost forgotten the pleasure to be found in flying across the water, the sails billowing in the wind, the tang of the salt spray in her face.

"I can't believe how many years it's been since I've been sailing," she said to Lucas.

Last night, when she'd been decked out in satins and lace, he'd thought Grace was the most beautiful woman he'd ever seen. Later, when he'd been making love to her by firelight, she'd been even more stunning.

But now, with her hair blown into a tousled cloud by the sea breeze, her exquisite face tinted pink by the sun, her arms outstretched as if she were about to fly off the bow of the boat, she was breathtaking.

"You've obviously been leading a deprived life."

Her laugh was rich and throaty and made him want to drag her belowdecks. "I think you just might be right."

"If you think this is fun, imagine how great it would be sailing out in the blue water. All the way up the coast to Alaska, Gracie. Just you and me, with the entire world in front of us and the wind at our backs."

"Lucas, please—"

"No." He held up his hand, forestalling what he knew was going to be a refusal. "Don't make up your mind yet. We've still got the rest of tonight. You can sleep on it, and give me your answer after the conference is over."

"But you'll still be going, won't you?" Because she didn't dare look at him when she asked this all-important question, Grace concentrated on where the sky met the water. "Whatever I decide."

Although he'd promised never to lie to her, Lucas wanted—needed—her to care enough, to love enough, to trust her heart.

"Yeah." He paused, choosing his words carefully, to protect her feelings as much as possible. "I've been in Sausalito longer than almost anywhere in my life. Someday I'll probably want to settle down in a house with a white picket fence and mow the lawn on Saturday mornings, hang out in my La-Z-Boy watching ESPN on Saturday afternoons and burn steaks in the backyard on Sundays. But I'm not there yet, Gracie."

Since he wanted her to make the decision on her own, he didn't reveal that if forced to, he'd behave like the pirate everyone seemed to think he was and kidnap her. He figured if he couldn't get her to forgive him by their first-month anniversary, he wasn't the man he saw in the mirror when he shaved each morning.

"Thank you." She managed a smile even as she felt her eyes misting up. "For being honest." She knew it would have been easier for him to lie, to tell her what she'd wanted to hear.

He caught her chin and turned her face back toward him. "If it makes you feel any better, you're the first woman who's ever made me consider tying up anchor." That was the absolute truth.

His words stayed with her the rest of the day. The more she thought about them, the more Grace suspected that perhaps, if she pulled out all the stops—if she agreed to marry him if only he'd agree to forgo his plans—he might change his mind.

But her victory would prove a shallow one, she knew, because eventually, perhaps years from now, he'd look back on this day and resent her. As he'd have every right to do.

A very strong part of Grace longed to just say yes, to throw caution to the wind and sail off to Alaska with Lucas, trusting in her heart. But although she'd written several romances using love-at-first-sight as a plot device, Grace couldn't quite believe in it. Despite Lucas's romantic tales about his family's history.

She'd made a bad choice once; how could she trust herself now? Even the undeniable fact that Lucas was nothing like Robert couldn't quite ease her concerns. Which was why Grace finally decided to put her worries away and bask in the golden pleasure of this near perfect day.

As much as she would have loved to stop the clock, the afternoon passed all too quickly, and soon it was time to get ready for the banquet. As she turned on the shower, Grace thought how much difference a few days could make. Although she'd won the ROMI three times before, on each previous occasion, Robert had been the one to accept the gold statuette, along with the applause and admiration of the romance community. But if Roberta Grace won tonight, Grace would also be standing on the stage. It would her moment in the sun.

Before she'd arrived in San Francisco, winning had been the uppermost thing in her mind. Now, with Lucas in her life, the award no longer seemed that important. Not nearly as important as the decision she would soon have to make. The decision that had her feeling more and more like Cinderella, with the hands of the clock racing toward midnight.

She was standing beneath the shower, enjoying the hot water sluicing over her body, when the glass door opened, allowing a billowing cloud of steam out and Lucas in.

"I thought, in the interests of saving water, I'd join you." As if it was the most normal thing in the world for him to be doing, he plucked the bar of soap from the shelf, rubbed it into a froth between his hands, then began spreading the luminescent bubbles over her breasts.

How was it that all it took was the touch of this man's hands on her body to make her head spin and her knees weak? "I'm all for conservation of precious resources," she managed to gasp as he lifted her up.

"Put your legs around me, Gracie." He pushed her back against the tile wall of the compact cubicle. Water was streaming over them, hot and pulsing. "Now take me, darlin'. Take all of me."

His hands were digging into her hips, his strong legs were braced wide apart to hold them both up, his mouth was racing over her face. "Oh, that's good," he murmured as she took him even deeper, her body tightening around his like a hot velvet fist. His teeth nipped at her neck and made her blood swim. "That's very, very good."

All it took was his mouth sucking hard on her breast to cause a responding pull in her center. When he scraped his teeth against a nipple, stimulating it to a point just this side of pain, the orgasm ripped through her. Feeling as if she'd been caught in an undertow, as if she was drowning, Grace could only grip his shoulders, nails biting into wet hot flesh as climax slammed into climax.

The water was hot. But Grace was hotter. As he felt her inner convulsions, Lucas felt as if his boiling blood was about to blast out of his veins. He covered her mouth with his as he drove harder, deeper, capturing her cry as he gave in to his own explosive release.

Together they sank to the tiled floor in a tangle of arms and legs as the shower continued to pelt down on them.

Grace drew in a ragged breath and felt as if her lungs were burning. "I may never move again."

"One of us is going to have to." He glanced up at the showerhead. "Before we run out of hot water."

Water streamed over her face as she followed his gaze. The faucet handles looked so very far away. "I should think that would be your job. Since you're the one supposedly taking care of my body." A job he'd done so magnificently well.

"Good point." Lucas pushed himself to his feet, twisted the chrome faucets and grabbed two fluffy towels from a heated rack right outside the door.

Not certain whether she was ready to try standing on her own, Grace willingly accepted his hand as he reached down and pulled her to her feet, then wrapped the over-size white towel around her. "Oh, it's warm." She snuggled into it.

"Only the best for America's most beloved romance writer."

Her smile touched her eyes as she met his teasing gaze. "Speaking of the best…"

She left the rest unsaid, but a man would have had to be blind not to read the message in those gleaming emerald eyes.

"So how long is this awards banquet supposed to last?" he asked.

She wrapped her arms around his waist. "Lucky for us, the award for best historical novel is early in the program."

"Lucky," he agreed, as he brushed her lips with his and wished that they were merely two ordinary people, getting ready for a night on the town. Unfortunately, their circumstances were far from ordinary.

As he left her to dress, Lucas was all too aware that someone was out to murder the woman he loved. And tonight would be the killer's last opportunity.

TINA WAS WAITING in the lobby when Grace and Lucas arrived.

"I have good news," she said to Grace in greeting. "I had drinks with George Dwyer earlier this evening. It was, all in all, a wonderfully productive meeting."

"Was Geraldine there?" Grace asked.

"No. But that doesn't matter. Because it seems that as editorial director, he's been given final approval on what Penbrook publishes."

"Is that standard operating procedure?" Lucas inquired.

"Darling, believe me, nothing is standard procedure in the publishing business. And you're right, it's a little unconventional, but then again, a diaper company publishing books isn't exactly the norm, either.

"Anyway, Grace," she said, smiling like a sleek Siamese that had just caught a very succulent pigeon, "he's agreed to everything. And even offered a higher advance than I'd expected for a three-book contract."

The number she revealed was nearly twice what Grace had dared hope for. "That's very generous."

"Generous, ha! You're worth it, darling. And the advertising budget is triple your previous ones. And here's the pièce de résistance. He's agreed to promise—in writing—that Penbrook will never publish a romance under the Roberta Grace name not written by either you or Robert, whoever wins the court case. Which of course will be you, once the facts are on record."

Since Grace refused to let herself believe that she wasn't going to win the court case, she felt as if an enormous load had just been taken from her shoulders.

"That is good news," she said, hugging the agent. "Thank you."

"You don't have to thank me, Grace," Tina said. "That's my job."

"Congratulations," Lucas said, as they continued walking across the lobby. "I take it this was what you wanted?"

"More than I wanted. And it's a relief to know that Penbrook still wants me."

"They'd be nuts if they didn't," Lucas said, giving her a slow, sexy smile that set her blood to simmering once more.

Grace heard her name being called again, and turned to

see Jamie headed her way, looking resplendent in a black silk maternity dress studded with jet bugle beads. Grace felt a stab of disloyalty as she found herself wondering what the evening gown must have cost.

"I just wanted to wish you good luck," her friend said, embracing her in what Grace knew had to be a genuine hug. "Not that you need it, of course."

"Thank you." Her emotions were on a roller coaster. Wasn't this conference bad enough without momentarily distrusting her best friend? She hugged Jamie back. "I love you," she said. Her eyes misted, her throat choked.

"Ditto," Jamie said. She backed up and touched a finger to her own moist eyes. "Now, go get 'em, girlfriend."

The awards banquet was held in the Golden Gate Ballroom, where the earlier attempt on Grace's life had taken place.

"You're wrong," Grace said as the entered the vast room. "Jamie's too good a friend to ever think about what you're accusing her of."

"She's only on the list, Grace. And not at the top. Especially since she didn't seem to be faking her affection."

"Of course she wasn't."

"On the other hand, those tears could have been the result of a guilty conscience," he suggested. "The same way yours were for momentarily doubting your best pal."

Grace wasn't entirely comfortable with the way Lucas seemed to be able to read her mind so well. "You don't know everything about me," she retorted archly.

"True. I figure we can work on that on the way to Alaska. And for the next fifty years or so. However, I do know that you're the most gorgeous woman in this hotel tonight."

His look, his deep drawl, which seemed to literally melt its way into her bones, the touch of his roughened fingertips against her cheek expunged Grace's brief irritation.

For tonight's festivities, the costume-pageant theater seating had been replaced with linen-draped tables adorned with elaborate floral centerpieces. Bottles of champagne were nestled into silver buckets on each of the tables, and sterling silver flutes, engraved with the RNN rose logo and this year's conference dates, graced each place setting. Up on the raised stage, a twelve-foot-tall, gold-painted figure of a woman—an oversize replica of the ROMI—looked down on the proceedings.

Although the shadows beneath the eyes of most of the RNN members revealed a lack of sleep these past nights, none of the writers appeared at all tired. On the contrary, the anticipation in the air was electric. This was the night they'd traveled from all parts of the globe to take part in, both the high point and the culmination of the three-day conference.

"I don't understand," Robert complained to the others seated at the table that had been reserved for the Penbrook Press group. "It's not like Buffy to disappear."

"Perhaps she finally got smart," Tina suggested dryly.

"That's right," he retorted, "when you can't think of anything constructive to say, fall back on sarcasm. With an attitude like that, I have to wonder about your negotiating skills."

"You never had any complaint before."

"Children, children," Geraldine chided, tapping her spoon against her crystal water goblet to get their attention. On the chair beside her, Dalai, resplendent in gold lamé for this stellar occasion, visibly perked up, as if hoping for some tidbit. "This is a special evening for all of us. Why don't we try to bury our individual hatchets for the time being?"

"I'd love to bury the hatchet," Tina drawled. "And I have just the idea where."

"That's it!" Robert threw down his napkin and was on

his feet in a shot. "I've had just about enough...oh, my god!"

The rest of the table followed his gaze to the doorway, where Buffy Cunningham Radcliffe stood, dressed in an oversize pair of jeans that bunched up around her feet, which were clad in oversize black rubber boots. A badly stained T-shirt hung down to her knees and what appeared to be kelp was tangled in her matted blond hair.

12

THE BUZZ OF CONVERSATION dropped off, table by table, as she made her way to the front of the banquet room.

"Buffy?" Robert went to take her in his arms, then noticeably backed away as he caught the pungent odor of fish emanating from her clothing. "What happened to you? I've been worried all day."

"What happened?" Her voice was ragged, but shrill. "What happened?" she repeated.

That she was on the verge of hysteria was more than a little apparent. Grace exchanged a look with Lucas, who shrugged his shoulders.

"Someone tried to kill me, that's what happened!"

"What are you talking about?" Lucas demanded. Grace felt his fingers tighten on hers. "When? How?"

"Last night. During the fireworks."

"I was looking all over the ship for you," Robert said.

"Well, you should have thought to look in the bay. Because that's where I was. After someone pushed me overboard."

"Surely you're mistaken," Geraldine said, her eyes wide. "Who on earth would want to kill you?"

"I can think of one person," Robert said, shooting an accusatory look at Grace.

"Watch it, Radcliffe," Lucas warned.

"You threw me across the ship's dining room," Grace's former husband countered hotly. "Why shouldn't we believe you'd be capable of throwing my wife into the bay?"

"That's reprehensible, even for you, Robert," Grace interjected hotly.

"Let me handle this, Gracie," Lucas said quietly. He turned back to Robert. "Not that I owe you any response, but I happen to be a bodyguard, not a hit man. And if you had anything but mush between your ears, you'd realize that the attack undoubtedly wasn't meant for your wife."

"Of course!" Geraldine said. "Both Buffy and Grace were wearing the same gown last night. And the night was dark and foggy—"

"Which made my would-be killer attack the wrong woman," Grace concluded.

"That'd be my guess," Lucas agreed. He stood up. "Let's get you out of here."

"No." Grace shook her head. "I'm not going to allow some horrible, sick person to control my life." She looked straight at Geraldine when she said it, receiving only a blank look in return.

"Dammit, Grace—"

"I'll be all right, Lucas. After all, you're here to protect me. And unless I'm mistaken, both Detectives MacDonald and Roberts seem to have suddenly developed an interest in romance fiction," she said, nodding toward the two detectives, who'd taken up positions at the stairs on either side of the raised stage. Undoubtedly at Lucas's request. "I'm probably as safe here as I'd be anywhere."

"I don't know, Grace," Geraldine said, "Lucas is a professional, and if he's concerned…"

"I'm not going," Grace repeated. She looked back up at Buffy, who'd been watching the exchange with a decided lack of interest. "It must have been terrible for you," she said. Although she had a great deal to resent her former editor for, never would she have wished such a horrendous experience on her. "How did you manage to survive?"

"I was picked up by a fishing boat."

"Which explains why you smell of mackerel," Robert said, wrinkling his nose. Dalai, on the other hand, was sniffing at Buffy's jeans with more than a little canine interest.

"Thank you for being so supportive, darling," Buffy drawled. "I'm certainly beginning to understand why Grace gave you up without a fight."

"I still don't understand," Geraldine pressed. "If you were picked up last night, where have you been all this time?"

"The boat's electrical system was out, so they couldn't get back to port. Which was fortunate, I suppose, since that's why they just happened to be sitting out there in the bay when I hit the water. Unfortunately, although I offered to foot the bill, the cheapskates refused to pay for a tug. So I was stuck there until they finally got the damn thing repaired."

"Do you remember anything about your attacker?" Lucas asked. "Height, weight, distinguishing characteristics…"

"I don't remember a thing except thinking I was going to die. And you and your cop pals can drag out all the bright lights and rubber hoses you want, but I categorically refuse to talk about last night—or think about it—anymore.

"As for you," she said, directing her words to Robert, "my lawyer will be contacting you after we get back to Manhattan." She pulled the ring off her finger, looked inclined to toss it onto the table, then apparently changed her mind.

"I believe I'll apply this to what you owe me. And don't try to use any of the credit cards, Robert. Because I'm canceling them all until a divorce court gives me my old life back. Or at least some of it," she amended, with an apologetic frown toward Grace.

She dragged a hand through her hair, dislodging seaweed. "And now, if you'll all excuse me, I'm going to go upstairs and take a long hot shower and try to remember why I didn't go into teaching."

"Far be it from me to interfere in someone else's marriage," Grace murmured as Buffy stomped back toward the double doors at the back of the banquet room. "But don't you think you should go after her, Robert?"

"I don't know." He appeared torn. "She said she'd like to be alone...."

"And you wouldn't want to miss the awards ceremony," Geraldine suggested dryly, her scorn evident to all.

"That's not it at all," he lied unconvincingly. Decision apparently made, he sat back down. "I know Buffy better than the rest of you. She just needs a little time alone to calm down. It's better that I stay here."

Not a single person challenged his self-centered behavior. Grace decided the others had come to the same conclusion she had—that he wasn't worth the effort.

"Georgie," Geraldine said, briskly changing the subject, "give Dalai some of your prime rib. The poor baby's hungry."

Lucas and Grace exchanged a brief look and tried not to smile as George dutifully did as instructed.

Surprisingly, although Grace could sense Lucas's heightened awareness, the rest of the meal passed in relative peace. Geraldine was surprisingly entertaining, spinning humorous tales about her days marketing disposable diapers to the Asian markets, and even George managed to make a joke or two about the family owing its fortune to wet baby bottoms.

"I suppose this is quite a change for you," Lucas suggested to Geraldine as the dinner plates were taken away and dessert served. "Moving from diapers to books."

"Actually, it's not," she said. "Romance novels are merely another market commodity—not that different from diapers, or soap, or even soup."

"Now there's a thought," Grace murmured. "Perhaps if I ever run into writer's block, I can just start mixing up chowder in my kitchen instead."

"You can scoff all you want, Grace," Geraldine chided in that brisk British accent that always reminded Grace of how the Queen should talk, but didn't. "But you creative types always have your head in the clouds, which makes you unable to understand the intricacies of the business world."

"How fortunate we have you to handle that for us," Grace murmured.

Her dry tone flew right over the publisher's head. "Isn't it?" Geraldine replied cheerfully. "But, of course, I could never write a book, either, so together we make a very good team."

Grace decided not to point out that the last time she'd been part of a writing team, her editor had stolen her husband.

"Just because we sell diapers doesn't mean that we don't appreciate good books," George said, entering into the conversation. "I've been meaning to tell you, Grace, that your hero in *Desperado* was the most heartbreakingly wonderful example of a wounded alpha male I've ever read."

"Why, thank you, George," Grace said, surprised by the idea that George Dwyer had actually read one of her books. When she'd learned that he'd been appointed editorial director, she'd believed, mistakenly, it seemed, that he'd only gotten the title due to nepotism. "I enjoyed writing him."

"I could tell. It came through on every page." He gave her a smile. "Actually, now that I think about it, there's quite a resemblance between Cole Remington and Lucas."

"How interesting you'd think that," Grace said pleasantly. Knowing the sexy, self-satisfied glint she'd see in Lucas's eyes, she refused to look at him.

The lights dimmed. The stage lights came on, signaling the beginning of the awards. Although winning a ROMI might mean less to her than it had three days ago, as she waited through the RNN president's closing remarks, and the announcement of the winner of the long series contemporary, and next, of the short series contemporary category—which Grace was thrilled turned out to be Jamie—her nerves began to tangle.

She was not alone. "I just wish they'd get to it," Robert grumbled as he reached over and took the chocolate mousse she'd been too nervous to eat. "I hate this waiting."

Grace, who hated to think there was anything she and the Rat might have in common, didn't answer.

And then it was her turn. She watched, cringing a little as a larger-than-life-size photograph flashed onto the huge screen along with a blowup of last year's Roberta Grace cover, featuring Kevin lounging seductively amid tangled sheets, a black Stetson on the bedpost, six-guns at his side.

"Oh, lord, he is gorgeous," Geraldine murmured. She leaned over to Grace. "Are you certain you want to change cover treatments?"

"Absolutely," Grace said firmly.

"It's such a waste," the publisher complained as the presenter began reading excerpts from each of the finalists' novels.

When the readings were finished, Lucas leaned toward

Grace from her other side. "You're a shoo-in," he assured her.

Her mouth had gone as dry as dust, preventing her from answering the encouraging vote of confidence. She could only squeeze his hand tighter.

"And the ROMI in the single-title historical category is awarded to…" The presenter paused, drawing out the moment.

Grace wasn't certain what happened next. One minute she was sitting on the edge of her chair, her fingernails digging into the back of Lucas's hand. The next minute, everything was pandemonium.

She was only vaguely aware of the woman on stage calling out Roberta Grace's name. At the same time, Robert suddenly turned a sickly purple hue, began choking and fell face first into what remained of the chocolate mousse he'd swiped from her.

Before Grace could fully absorb what had happened, Lucas was on his feet, his Beretta drawn. "Let's go." Giving her no chance to argue, he dragged her out a side exit as the detectives just as quickly headed toward the table.

They took the service elevator. Grace's head was still spinning as they entered the suite. Her heart was pounding like a tom-tom; her legs were so rubbery she wasn't certain she'd be able to stand were it not for Lucas's arm around her waist.

"Are you all right?"

"Yes. I think. Thanks to you."

"The job isn't over yet. I've got to get back down there, in case whoever poisoned your dessert tries to get away." His eyes were as hard as obsidian, his jaw was firm, a muscle jerked in his cheek. "I want to make certain we end this right here. Tonight."

He ran a palm over her shoulder in an unsuccessful attempt to soothe. Then went over to the bar and poured a generous splash of brandy into a balloon glass. "Here, sweetheart." He pressed the glass into her trembling hands. "Given my history, I'm usually not one to recommend drinking, but I think in this case it's excusable."

With her eyes on his, Grace took a tentative sip and felt the liquor warming the chill that seemed to have seeped into every molecule of her body.

"I want you to stay here," he said. "Whatever you do, don't open the door for anyone except me. Okay?"

Because she was afraid her voice would come out all shaky, Grace simply nodded.

"Good girl." He bent down, gave her a swift, hard kiss. And then he was gone, leaving Grace to wonder, not for the first time, how this could possibly be happening to her.

She was sitting there, nerves still tangled as she waited for Lucas to return and tell her that everything was all right, that she was going to have her normal, boring life back again, when there was a knock on the door. She froze.

Another knock. Grace debated going over to look out the door's peephole, but was unreasonably afraid of being seen by whoever was on the other side.

"Grace," the familiar voice called to her. "It's me. Jamie. Are you all right?"

Grace jumped to her feet and looked out, confirming that it was, indeed, her best friend. Lucas's warning about not opening the door to anyone flashed through her mind, but this was Jamie. The one person besides Lucas she could trust. Despite whatever financial problems the Winstons might be experiencing.

"Just a minute," she called out as she hurried to unfasten the chain. She'd no sooner opened the door than Jamie literally fell across the threshold, pushed into the room by Geraldine.

"I'm sorry, Grace." Tears flooded from Jamie's distressed eyes. "I didn't want to do it, but she's got my Susie."

"Susie?" Grace didn't know which she found more shocking—the sight of her new publisher holding that horrid chrome pistol or the idea of Geraldine snatching Grace's seven-year-old goddaughter. "How? Where?"

"Back home. I talked to her on the phone just a minute ago. Although we've told her time and time again not to talk to strangers, she thought she was trying to help the nice man find his lost cocker spaniel puppy."

"Oh, Jamie, no!"

"They threatened to do horrible things to her if I didn't cooperate," Jamie sobbed. "I'm so, so sorry."

"Don't worry about it." Grace trusted Lucas to save her. The key, she determined, was to get Geraldine talking. "How could you do such an evil thing?"

"I didn't want to. I wanted to keep this just between the two of us," the publisher revealed. There was a wild look in her eyes that Grace could only view as madness. "But then you ruined things by hiring yourself a bodyguard. So, naturally, I realized I needed a backup plan. Just in case."

Her smile was cold, rather like the way a rattler would look if a snake could smile. "I knew that other than the hunk, there was only one person in the world you'd trust. But that led to another problem, because there was also no way your best friend would betray you.

"But then I saw her showing off snapshots of her family to friends and I realized right away what I had to do."

"Kidnapping and threatening a child is abhorrent," Grace said.

"Oh, we haven't threatened her. Actually, she's being treated very well, with videos and all the candy and ice cream she can eat. So long as her mother cooperates," she added evilly.

"I still don't understand," Grace complained. "I've never done anything to hurt you. Why would you want to kill me?"

Before Geraldine could answer, the door opened again and George Dwyer walked into the suite. He was still carrying Dalai, but Grace noticed that for the first time since she'd seen the dog, it wasn't wearing a costume. Although to her mind, it still looked more like a mop than a real dog.

"I think I can answer that," he said.

"How did you get a key?" Geraldine demanded.

"I simply asked a maid. I told her I'd lost mine. Apparently she thought I looked as if I belonged in the presidential suite. Unlike some other people I could mention," he said, his voice edged with sarcasm, his words meant for Penbrook's new publisher.

"Geraldine was having an affair with my father," he told Grace. "When she began demanding that he leave my mother, he realized she'd become obsessive. So, since he'd just bought Penbrook—at my suggestion, by the way—" he revealed, "he named her publisher to get her out of the Dwyer's Diapers building. But I was assured full editorial control."

"That's what the checks were for," Grace said, as comprehension dawned.

"What checks?" Jamie asked. Although tears were still streaming down her cheeks, she seemed interested in the story.

"Checks from George Senior that Geraldine deposited in her personal account," Grace said. "You were blackmailing him, weren't you?" The grandfather clock chimed the hour. *Keep the crazy woman talking*, Grace told herself. Lucas would arrive in time; she could not allow herself to think otherwise.

"Blackmail's such an ugly word," Geraldine said. "I prefer to think of it as payment for services rendered. Very personal services," she added, with an insinuating smile George's way.

"Father never would have left mother for you," George said. "Not with my mother owning fifty-one percent of Dwyer's Diapers' stock. He might have fallen prey to whatever seduction tactics you used to worm your way into the executive offices, but he would never have given up control of that voting block. Besides, my parents' relationship might not exactly be Ozzie and Harriet, but it works quite well for them."

"I still don't understand what this has to do with me," Grace complained. "Or why you were manipulating my royalties."

"Ah, you and your hunk *have* been busy, haven't you?" Geraldine gave Grace another of those cold, eerie smiles. "You're Penbrook's cash cow, darling. I thought if I skimmed a little from your account, cooked the numbers a bit, you'd get disillusioned with Penbrook's plummeting royalties and leave. But then, when it looked as if you were actually thinking of staying, and it became obvious you were going to win that silly lawsuit Robert instigated, well, naturally, I had to employ more drastic measures."

The door between the suite and the adjoining room opened. "Like killing the writer who penned the golden romances," Lucas drawled, seeming unfazed by the sight of Geraldine holding the others at gunpoint.

"Dammit! This is getting like Grand Central Station!" Geraldine shouted. She grabbed Grace's arm with one hand. With the other she pressed the pistol against her temple. "If you so much as move a muscle, I'll kill her," she warned Lucas.

"Hey." He lifted his hands in the air. "It's your call. Just let's try to calm down and—"

"I don't need to calm down!" she shrieked. Grace flinched, then shut her eyes, expecting to die at that moment. "I just need something to go right for a change."

"You don't want to do this," Lucas said.

"Now there's where you're wrong. Unfortunately, I had the misfortune to hire the world's most inept hit man." She shook her head. "First he misses when he shoots at her. Then the idiot throws the wrong woman overboard…. But tonight's plan was supposed to be foolproof. And it would have worked, if Robert hadn't been such a damn greedy pig."

Grace's blood chilled as she realized her dessert truly had been poisoned. But so long as Geraldine was talking, she wasn't shooting. Which was definitely in Grace's favor.

"You'll never get away with this," Lucas said in a calm, matter-of-fact tone. Although he was more terrified than he'd been that fateful night on the beach, when he'd believed *he* was about to die, he forced himself, for Grace's sake, to remain coolheaded.

"You've got too many witnesses. And even if you're willing to risk killing us all, that will eliminate most of the other suspects, which will lead the cops straight to you. And then there's the little fact that you've left a paper trail even Barney Fife could follow."

"I moved that money through three off-shore banks," Geraldine retorted. "There shouldn't have been any way to track it." She glared at him. "Obviously, I made a mistake in underestimating you. But what kind of bodyguard can anyone expect to find in the classifieds, anyway?" she asked in a scathing tone.

"The very best," Grace said, experiencing another flash of her newly discovered temper. "You might as well face it, Geraldine, Lucas is smarter than you'll ever be. And he's not going to let you get away with this."

"Grace…" Lucas murmured.

"I'm sorry, Lucas. I might be going to die, but I refuse to allow this horrible person to insult you like that."

"Isn't that sweet," Geraldine drawled scathingly. "No wonder you write the kind of stories you do. You're a romantic." She heaped an extra helping of derision on the term.

Her hand had begun to shake. Lucas judged the distance between them and decided he didn't dare risk making a move. Yet.

"That's true," Grace agreed. "And I'm proud of it. Face it, Geraldine, you're just jealous because no one could ever love such an evil, self-absorbed woman. You treated sex with George Senior like a business deal, and you ended up emotionally bankrupt. And, for the record, you may have been great at pushing diapers, but you don't understand anything about publishing."

"And you think Georgie here could do better?" Geraldine asked with a contemptuous laugh. "He's a sentimental bleeding heart who mistakenly believes that the business is still about telling stories."

"It isn't?" Lucas asked mildly.

"Of course not. It's a jungle. It's survival of the fittest and only the strongest survive."

"You're wrong," George said, surprising Grace by standing up to his tormentor yet again.

"Oh, shut up, Georgie." Geraldine cut him off. "No one cares what you have to say."

"Shut up yourself, you old witch!" he shouted at her. "You climbed the corporate ladder on your back, lady, and I'm sick of having to listen to your idiot marketing schemes that have nothing to do with what books are about. And I'm sick of lighting your damn cigarettes, and you know what I'm also sick of?'' His voice kept going higher and higher, like an operatic tenor practicing scales. "I'm sick to death of the way you've turned this innocent dog into this ill-behaved, ridiculous, gas-filled bag of mangy fur!" That said, he flung Dalai at her.

Geraldine's hand instinctively came up, whether to protect herself from the flying Lhasa apso or, in an uncharacteristic gesture of protection, to catch it to prevent it from hitting the floor. Whichever, Lucas took advantage of the opportunity and made his move.

As publisher, dog and bodyguard went tumbling to the floor, Grace immediately grabbed a sterling candlestick from the coffee table and threw herself into the melee, hitting the other woman wherever she could land a blow, determined to protect Lucas from Geraldine's deadly gun.

"Grace, it's okay." Jamie was pulling her off the pile. "Everything's under control. It's all over."

At the same time, Lucas pushed himself to his feet, pulling Geraldine with him.

"You're wrong," Grace corrected softly as she looked straight into the eyes of the man she'd fallen in love with. "It's just beginning."

SUNDAY DAWNED BRIGHT and clear, the waters of the bay and the Pacific beyond gleaming like newly mined sapphires. Grace stood beside Lucas as they sailed the *Rebel's Reward* beneath the Golden Gate, headed toward blue water.

"So, what did your mother say about attending the wedding in Anchorage?" he asked.

"She said she was looking forward to the adventure." Grace had been surprised and pleased by her mother's instant acceptance.

"That's pretty much what my folks said, too. Oh, and it

turns out Fancy has read all your books—she called them keepers, by the way—and I'm supposed to tell you she's bringing them with her to be autographed."

"That's sweet." Grace smiled.

"So, I think everything's set…damn."

"What?"

"I forgot. There's one more thing I have to do before we get out of cell range." He pulled out the compact phone and punched a local number. "Hey, Samantha, sweetheart, I've got a going away present for you. I've found my replacement. His name's Jackson Beaumont. Here's his number." He repeated it twice. "He's a former SEAL—in fact, he's the guy who led the team that broke me out of that hellhole in the Caribbean. And believe it or not, Beaumont's almost as handsome as me. Trust me, Sam, you're going to flat-out love him."

The last of the loose ends tied up, Lucas closed the phone, put his arm around Grace's waist and pulled her close against him as he turned the ketch up the coast.

"Next stop, Alaska," he said.

"And then the world."

Feeling more carefree and happy than she ever had in her life, Grace lifted her face to the wind as they sailed together into their future.

The door to Maddie's bedroom crashed open.

SHE SAT UP on the bed and rubbed at her watery eyes, her heart leaping into her throat. When she'd made her escape from the parlor fifteen minutes before, she'd hoped that Jack would just get in his car and leave.

"Where is it?" Jack's voice filled the room, as intimidating as his figure in the doorway. In the low light of the setting sun, she couldn't see his features. She didn't need to see his face to know that he was angry.

"Go away," she cried, throwing an embroidered pillow in his direction.

"What did you do with him, Maddie?"

"With who?"

"Lamar! He didn't just get up and crawl out of that coffin!"

Maddie's heart did a back flip. She scrambled off the huge bed and smoothed her wrinkled skirt only to grab it up in her clenched fists. "You—you opened Lamar's coffin?"

"What did you do with him? Did you hide the body? Or maybe there never *was* a body in there. Maybe you disposed of poor Lamar long ago. Tossed him in the river or buried him in the rose garden." Jack stepped inside the room, closing the door behind him. "No wonder there was never an autopsy."

Maddie walked over to the open french doors and

stared out into the growing darkness, her nerves jangling, her heart thudding. "There was no autopsy because there never was a body," she said, her back to Jack.

"Yeah, right. Now you're going to tell me that Lamar simply decomposed more quickly than your average corpse. I've heard all the stories about what an extraordinary man he was, but I don't think even *he* could have managed that."

Maddie turned and shook her head, surprised by the thread of jealousy she detected in Jack's voice. "I think it's time I ex—"

Her words were drowned out by the sound of glass and wood shattering near her ear. A spray of splinters and shards of glass stung her bare shoulder. Maddie cried out and an instant later, she found herself on the floor, Jack lying on top of her. She shook her head, trying to rid herself of the ringing in her ears. Birds had flown through the open french doors before, but they'd never broken a window.

"That must have been a big bird," she said, stunned and confused, listening for the flapping of wings.

"Don't move," Jack warned.

He lay on top of her for a long time, long enough for her to realize she couldn't breathe. "Will you get off me," she said, wriggling beneath him. "It was just a bird!"

"Dammit, Maddie, hold still!"

She shoved against his shoulders. "If this is some new method of seduction, I don't like it! My arm is falling asleep and there's something digging into my—"

Jack clapped his hand over her mouth. "Quiet!"

She pried his fingers off his mouth. "I will not be—"

"Maddie," Jack warned, looking darkly into her eyes. *"That was a gunshot."*

Glamorous, hot, seductive...

THE AUSTRALIANS

Stories of romance Australian-style guaranteed to
fulfill that sense of adventure!

September 1998, look for
Playboy Lover
by **Lindsay Armstrong**

When Rory and Dominique met at a party the attraction was
magnetic, but all Dominique's instincts told her to resist him.
Not easy as they'd be working together in the steamy tropics
of Australia's Gold Coast. When they were thrown together in
a wild and reckless experience, obsessive passion flared—but
had she found her Mr. Right, or had she fallen for yet another
playboy?

*The Wonder from Down Under: where spirited women win
the hearts of Australia's most independent men!*

Available September 1998 at your favorite retail outlet.

HARLEQUIN®
Makes any time special ™

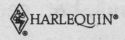

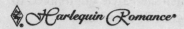

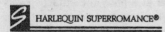

MEN at WORK

All work and no play?
Not these men!

July 1998

MACKENZIE'S LADY by Dallas Schulze

Undercover agent Mackenzie Donahue's
lazy smile and deep blue eyes were his best
weapons. But after rescuing—and kissing!—
damsel in distress Holly Reynolds, how could
he betray her by spying on her brother?

August 1998

MISS LIZ'S PASSION by Sherryl Woods

Todd Lewis could put up a building with ease,
but quailed at the sight of a classroom! Still,
Liz Gentry, his son's teacher, was no battle-ax,
and soon Todd started planning some
extracurricular activities of his own....

September 1998

A CLASSIC ENCOUNTER
by Emilie Richards

Doctor Chris Matthews was intelligent, sexy
and *very* good with his hands—which made
him all the more dangerous to single mom
Lizette St. Hilaire. So how long could she
resist Chris's special brand of TLC?

Available at your favorite retail outlet!

MEN AT WORK™

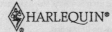 

Look us up on-line at: http://www.romance.net   PMAW2

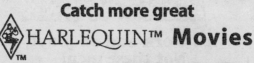

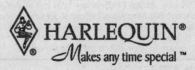

COMING NEXT MONTH

#697 A BODY TO DIE FOR Kate Hoffmann
Hero for Hire

When bodyguard Jackson Beaumont discovered he'd be guarding Judge Lamar Parmentier, he never suspected the judge was a corpse! Or that the late judge's widow would be so young, so gorgeous, so irresistible.... But Madeline Parmentier had a secret. And until Jackson figured out what she was hiding, he didn't dare trust her with his heart—or his life!

#698 TAKEN! Lori Foster
Blaze

Virginia Johnson ran a huge corporation—she was a woman in control. Until Dillon Jones—whose job description *wasn't* listed in the Fortune 500—kidnapped her. Suddenly she was at the mercy of a powerfully sexy man who kept her both captive...and captivated.

#699 SINGLE SHERIFF SEEKS... Jo Leigh
Mail Order Men

Single sheriff Dan Collins was seeking some peace and quiet. That ended when the townsfolk placed his personal ad in *Texas Men* magazine. Coincidentally, Dan stumbled upon his most bizarre case ever—and one very single sexy suspect. What could Dan do but stick *closer-than-this* to gorgeous Annie Jones?

#700 THE LAST BACHELOR Carolyn Andrews

Mac Delaney couldn't believe it—he'd lost all his poker buddies to matrimony! But Mac wasn't about to let any woman drag him to the altar *ever*. Then he met gorgeous Frankie Carmichael, and was ready to kiss the single life goodbye...till he discovered Frankie had *no* desire to walk down the aisle either!

AVAILABLE NOW:

#693 1-800-HERO
JoAnn Ross
#694 THE PRINCESS AND THE P.I.
Donna Sterling

#695 SINGLE IN THE SADDLE
Vicki Lewis Thompson
#696 SUMMER HEAT
Pamela Burford and Patricia Ryan